Ekrem and the Secrets of the Seven Cities

L. G. MorGan

This book is dedicated to:

* My amazing family who have encouraged and supported me in producing this book and for their ongoing love, generosity and faithfulness, not just to me but to the many people they love, serve and care for every day. You are such treasures!

* Tacim Gunduz and Bediş, their two sons, Arda and Cagan, and their niece, Dila. You are wonderful people, and it has been an honour and a pleasure to meet you.

* Some incredible friends who have given their lives to serve people all over the world, including: Alli Blair, Steve and Esther Uppal, Simon Guillebaud, and, Marcus and Andrea Enzenebner.

*

Chapter 1

When Ekrem's parents told him that his grandfather had died, he was quite distraught. He had been very fond of Grandpa with whom he had spent time learning about the history of their nation, Turkey. Grandpa had been a historian, but not the sort that sometimes seemed quite boring to a thirteen-year-old boy, but one that had managed to make history come alive through drama, storytelling and archaeological artefacts that he had collected over the years.

'But your grandfather has left you some of his greatest treasures in his will,' Ekrem's mother explained. 'They are due to be delivered here in Kusadasi tomorrow.'

Ekrem's brain had spent the rest of the day anticipating what treasures were going to arrive. He knew that Grandpa had always collected things, but he now imagined treasure boxes of gold coins; crowns of gold from kings of the past; ancient treasures that would be worth millions of Turkish kurus; and expensive perfumes, oils and fragrances made from years ago. The excitement grew so much that Ekrem couldn't resist trampolining on the bed until there was a splitting sound of wood that resonated all the way downstairs, followed by his mother's voice enquiring as to what he had broken now.

'Nothing,' lied Ekrem, trying to hastily repair the wooden bar underneath the mattress that had come away from one end of his bed. *Superglue is good for a quick repair job,* he thought, although he knew that it would not stay repaired for much longer than twenty-four hours at best.

*

The next day at school, Ekrem just couldn't hold back telling all of the people in his history class that he was receiving treasures later in the day. He knew that his mind was telling him to be wise and keep the information to himself, but his mouth was far too excited to be quiet.

'It probably won't be that brilliant,' scoffed Emir from across the other side of the room. 'You'll probably just end up with some bits of old stones and broken pottery pieces from years ago.'

'No, I reckon it will be some hideous piece of clothing that no-one now-a-days would want to be seen wearing in a million years,' retorted Hamza, who always enjoyed the opportunity to put other people down.

'Or some old pieces of jewellery which really would have been worn by women, not boys,' laughed Narin, pretending to mime out putting the jewellery around her own neck.

Ekrem was not moved by their comments. 'What if it was a treasure chest full of gold coins?' he started.

'Then it would be in the Topkapi Palace Museum in Istanbul,' said Emir, 'not in your grandfather's house!'

Good point thought Ekrem. *Maybe I am over-thinking this treasure just a little too much. Okay, forget the treasure chest of old coins, but there still might be lots of other rich and beautiful things.*

The delivery arrived at about 5:20pm that afternoon. Ekrem and his younger sister, Alida, had been gazing out of the window waiting ever since he had arrived home from school. *Time goes by incredibly slowly when you are waiting for something exciting,* he contemplated to himself. *I wonder why this is. It goes by too fast when you're having fun, but too slowly whilst waiting. Mind you, it goes slowly when you're in the dentist chair as well...I guess you could say that even being in the dentist chair is a kind of waiting game.*

Ekrem watched the delivery men get out of the lorry and open the back. He anticipated lots and lots of boxes to come out, but instead there was just two items. One was just a very long tube (about two metres long) and the other one was a cuboid box that was just fractionally longer and wider than an A4 pack of paper. *Hmm...*

Both he and Alida dashed down the stairs and just beat their father by a few seconds to opening the front door.

"Hi," Ekrem called out to the delivery men, "I believe those things are for me."

The first delivery man, who was big built, muscular and with a long black moustache, turned to look at him, his eyebrow raised. "Is it?" he asked. "We shall have to see about that."

"He is rather excited," called out Ekrem's father, watching the second man, who was the skinnier of the two, try to lift out the long tube by himself.

The first man handed over the small box and turned to look at his assistant. "He'll get some muscles one day," he said, "if I keep him working hard like this."

The second man came staggering up before half-throwing, half-dropping the tube onto the floor, narrowly missing Ekrem's foot.

"What is it?" asked Ekrem.

"I don't know!" laughed the big man. "It doesn't come from me now, does it? You're the one who's supposed to know what's in it!"

*

Minutes later, the packages were in the living room. In Ekrem's mind, it didn't seem right to rush into opening them as you might a present at the Muslim festival of Eid al-Fitr. Perhaps this was out of respect for Grandpa, but in another sense, Ekrem didn't want to be disappointed with what he might find inside the packages. *What if his friends had been right?*

His sister, Alida, on the other hand was a total opposite. Presents were there to be opened so why wait. After all, Grandpa had left them to be enjoyed, not sat in wrapping on the living room floor. "Come on, Ekrem," Alida said. "We can't stand here all evening just staring at two packages. Let's see what Grandpa has left you. Okay?"

Ekrem nodded. *We'll start with the little box,* he thought, reaching out his hand to take hold of one end to open it.

As he removed the packaging, there emerged a box file, the kind that are normally kept in offices for pieces of paper. Ekrem had seen similar ones in the school office. He opened it to find an envelope addressed to him with piles of old papers underneath it.

The papers were scribbled notes about all sorts of complicated, historical things with diagrams that looked impossible to understand. Ekrem's heart sank. *How very disappointing. Perhaps the tube would be better?* His parents could tell that he was upset.

The tube was extremely heavy. It required a lot of effort even from his father to open the packaging around it. As the plastic sheeting was removed out of the way, it became apparent that it was an incredibly old Turkish rug. Ekrem and his father unrolled it. The design of it was weird with seemingly no shape and strange symbols scattered in...one, two, three, four, five, six... seven parts of the rug. Ekrem walked around it several times looking at it from different angles, but it didn't seem to be very attractive whichever direction you stared at it. It was a little threadbare and covered in quite a lot of dust. It clearly hadn't been on a floor for a long, long time.

The disheartened Ekrem sat on the sofa with his chin resting on his hands, just gazing at the top of the items with a sense of disbelief. *Was this it? Were these the great treasures that Grandpa had sent him? What about all the other marvellous things he had seen in Grandpa's house before? Where had they gone?*

"Are you going to open the card?" his mother asked him.

Ekrem shook his head. "I hardly think there's going to be millions of Turkish kurus in there."

*

The card itself had actually turned out to be quite intriguing although it hadn't been until the next morning that Ekrem had shaken himself out of his miserable mood and actually started reading it.

Dear Ekrem,

Over the many times you have been to visit me, I have shown you many of the wonderful things I have had the opportunity to collect; but the greatest items I have never shown you are now being sent to you. Not only are these items valuable and unique, but they also contain the secrets of seven cities, which will give you the greatest treasures you will ever know. I am also sending an expert to help you uncover the secrets. I know that you will be extremely excited as you find these things.

Finally, remember that treasures and secrets of this kind are reserved for the wise, so be sensible and prudent with all that you find. Don't throw your pearls before swine.

Remember me always.

Grandpa.

Ekrem read it repeatedly. *What a lot to think about,* he thought to himself, *and what does it all mean?*

*

"I saw your delivery lorry arrive yesterday," said Mehmet in the school playground. "It didn't look like very much arrived to me, certainly nothing very exciting."

Mehmet was the annoying boy who lived on the other side of the road. His parents were extraordinarily successful businesspeople whom Ekrem thought had more money than sense as well as having an irritating child such as Mehmet.

"So..." started Mehmet again tauntingly, "what were these great treasures you received? I see you're not wearing any golden crown today, King Ekrem?"

"Oh, go and bury your head back in the sand, Mehmet," Ekrem replied, trying to hold back the frustration and anger.

"So, we were right then, were we?" continued Mehmet. "No gold coins? No golden crowns? No fine jewellery?"

"Not yet," muttered Ekrem.

Mehmet let out a loud and high pitched heckle. "Not yet? Is that all you can say? There's going to be no more, Ekrem. That was your delivery, remember? There's no more coming!"

Ekrem's hand was beginning to clench and every muscle wanted to thump Mehmet right on the nose, not just for now, but for every irritating comment he had ever said since the dawn of time. He was saved from doing so by the bell, telling them that the school day was about to start.

*

It hadn't been any easier from any of his friends in the class who had all laughed at him and mocked him for not being Kusadasi's next millionaire. But Ekrem knew deep on the inside that there had to be something special about the rug and the papers. Also, Grandpa had mentioned about sending an expert so the things can't have been junk. Things would work out all right in the end and then his friends would stop laughing.

*

It was later that afternoon that the doorbell rang and yet another package arrived. Ekrem ran down the stairs to answer it. Outside, the courier stood there holding a small-ish box that once again was addressed to Ekrem and in the same handwriting to the deliveries that had arrived yesterday.

"Parcel for you," said the delivery man. "Obvious, I know, but that's what they tell me I have to say. Sign here, please."

Ekrem took the pen and signed the machine, before closing the door and taking it into the living room.

"Another parcel from Grandpa," he said. "But what could it be?"

Chapter 2

Ekrem stared in disbelief. The parcel simply had seven candles inside of it, all with their own matching saucers to sit on. On the side of the candles were strange letters that Ekrem had certainly never seen before.

"They must be some sort of language," he said to his father.

"Well, you will have to do some research on the Internet," his father replied. "It shouldn't take too much work to find various alphabets on there."

Hmm... thought Ekrem. *But why send these in a separate package? You would have thought that all the belongings would have arrived together.*

Ekrem's sister, Alida, walked into the room. "Ooh, candles," she said. "And they've got Hebrew writing on them."

"How do you know that?" replied Ekrem.

"Because we have been learning about Judaism in R.E. at school," answered Alida. "I recognise the writing."

"So, what does it say?" enquired Ekrem, hoping that his younger sister might have paid enough attention in her lessons to remember what the letters actually said."

"Sorry, I can't remember. We could look it up though."

Ekrem fetched his I-pad and quickly looked up on the Internet the Jewish alphabet. (Otherwise known as the Hebrew alphabet.)

The answers came quite quickly. There were two letter 'S', two letter 'P', one 'L', one 'E', and one 'T'.

"It must spell something," said Ekrem curiously. He and Alida sat together at the table with the candles moving them about from one position to another to see what words they could make.

"Perhaps, we are doing this all wrong," suggested Alida. "We're trying to think of Turkish words, but the letters are in Hebrew, so maybe it's a Hebrew word."

Good thought, pondered Ekrem, wishing that he himself had worked this out rather than his twelve-year-old sister. *Being one year older than her should make him smarter, shouldn't it?*

His mother quickly changed the subject. "Have either of you thought about why Grandpa sent these items to Ekrem?"

"Actually... why did Ekrem get things and not me?" suddenly asked Alida. "I used to see him too sometimes."

"You were never interested in his historical collections, Alida," Ekrem's father answered seriously. "You were more interested in Geography, mainly people and places."

"Well... history is of the past. Geography is about people living in places in the here and now," replied Alida.

*

After dinner, Ekrem returned to his room, closed the door and left Alida talking to his parents in the living room. *These presents are all very strange - weird somehow – some paperwork, a rug with strange patterns on it, and now, Hebrew candles.* He lay back on his bed, turned on the I-pad and started playing the game 'Hızlı sürüş', a favourite of his in which he normally won gold.

There was a knock at the door and his mother walked into the room. "Ekrem, do you want to come down and listen to what your father has worked out about the rug? He has just laid it out on the floor and it's fascinating. Alida is coming down too."

"I am on my way," Ekrem replied excitedly. Nothing would normally distract him from his game, but this could not be missed.

Alida came dashing along the corridor, full of enthusiasm, brushing her long brown, curly hair. "Aren't you excited, Ekrem?" she asked.

I think so, thought Ekrem. "Yes," he replied. "I am. I'll be downstairs in a few minutes."

*

The rug had been spread out on the living room floor. It looked threadbare in many places with its colours extremely faded and with no symmetry about it whatsoever. On one side seemed to be a jagged line whilst the opposite long side had a straight-ish line. There were some bright yellow circles in seven random places across the rug surrounded by strange symbols and pictures, some of which seemed to symbolise some animals, but Ekrem couldn't be sure. It certainly didn't seem like a normal Turkish rug. *Perhaps it's also from another culture,* Ekrem thought. *It's not exactly the nicest thing I have ever seen.*

His father was stood in front of the drinks' cabinet, looking at the family from the opposite side of the rug. "The rug is the correct way up from your direction," he started. "It's upside down to me, but I can still explain."

For the next hour or so, he proceeded to tell Ekrem and Alida about how the strange shape that followed the majority of the edge of the rug was indeed a replica of a map dating back to the Roman era of the western coast of Turkey. He brought out a paper copy from the file Grandpa had sent.

"So it is," said Ekrem's mother, who was now completely fascinated.

"It says here that the seven circles are symbolic of seven important cities during the Roman era," his father continued. "All of these cities were extremely influential and significant in passing trade through the Roman Empire. Turkey was the doorway between Europe and the Middle East. Without Turkey the Roman Empire would have been split into two sections, but because of its geographical location, it became highly strategic and therefore highly profitable. The seven cities therefore were vital."

Ekrem listened intently. This was certainly the best history lesson he had had in a long time.

"But Grandpa also mentioned about secrets?" he eventually asked.

Oh, I don't know about any secrets," said his father. "There's nothing in the paperwork from Grandpa about secrets."

"So, it's just a boring old rug," groaned Ekrem, who now had completely forgotten his excitement from earlier and was now frankly disappointed.

Ekrem thanked his father for the information about the rug and went up to his room. Alida stayed with their parents, contemplating if there was any significance between the candles and the rug. *Perhaps it was just Grandpa's living room items,* she thought.

*

'Who was the extra present for?" asked Mehmet the next day at school.

"What present?" replied Ekrem, only half awake from having overslept through the alarm clock.

"The one that arrived at your house last night dropped off by the courier," Mehmet replied.

Ekrem's brain suddenly remembered.

"Do you spy on everything?" Ekrem replied, feeling quite indignant that nothing could happen without 'Mystery Mehmet' knowing all about it. It was like being spied on by MI5 or something. *Anyway, he doesn't know what the items were or any of their significance,* he thought to himself, *I don't know why he needs to know about it all anyway.* "Shouldn't you try and get a life of your own?" he answered cruelly.

"No, yours is much more interesting," replied Mehmet, who always had an answer for everything. "When things arrive at my house, we open them up and I know what they are; but when things happen at other peoples' houses, that's when I don't know what they are and so it makes it more intriguing. By the way, did I tell you about..."

He continued talking on and on and on, but Ekrem's ears had already switched off from the continual drone of Mehmet's voice.

"So, do I get to come round and see the items sometime?" asked Mehmet.

"I doubt it," Ekrem replied. "There's only a rug, some candles and a box of papers."

Blow it! thought Ekrem. *I have just given away what the items were. I wasn't thinking. At least it sounds boring enough that Mehmet won't want to see anymore.*

*

Ekrem couldn't focus his mind for the rest of the day at school. The lessons all seemed boring and even his favourite school lunch of Tavuc Durum (chicken doners) didn't appeal too much. There were just two things on his mind: first, the rug and the secrets that it seemingly held; and second, treasure. *Grandpa had said something about treasure, hadn't he?*

*

When he reached home, no-one was there. His mother had apparently gone out to buy some matches. *I guess she's going to light the candles at mealtime or something,* he thought to himself.

Ekrem walked into the living room. Perhaps there would be an answer to this rug and candles that he just hadn't thought about yet. There, on the sideboard, nearest the fireplace were the seven candles, six short ones and one tall one in the middle. They were white and gold. He was just about to pick one up when he heard the key in the front door lock. He dashed over to the sofa, switched on the TV and proceeded to watch the programme innocently. His mother came in the room.

"You got some matches then," he said, noticing the box in her hand.

"Yes, thank you," she replied. "Did you have a good day at school?"

"Err...well..." started Ekrem who had been caught completely off guard. "It was quite a boring day really. Lots of uninteresting lessons from dry, dull teachers. Not the same as father's talk last night..."

"Yes, that was interesting," his mother replied. "Have you had any more thoughts about it, Ekrem?"

"No," he replied. "Besides which, I am busy this evening."

Busy?! Busy doing what? Playing computer games? His mother would never believe that lame excuse.

"Well, your father says he can't tell us anymore about the rug this evening. He needs to go through the paperwork more thoroughly," his mother explained.

"Well, if he's busy, he's busy," Ekrem replied. "Perhaps I ought to go through all Grandpa's paperwork to sort it out. I am not being impatient, but we need to know more, don't we?!"

His mother couldn't disagree. She seemed delight that Ekrem was taking a fresh interest in the items.

*

The evening passed by quite quickly. Ekrem had spent most of it scrambling through pieces of paper that didn't seem to make a lot of sense. The only interesting one seemed to be that the candles came with the rug. *Seven candles, seven circles...* Ekrem's brain suddenly made a connection. *The candles go on the circles of the rug.* He was about to go and tell his parents but decided that it might sound a bit silly. *After all, who puts candles on a rug?*

At about 9pm Ekrem went upstairs to bed. To his surprise a piece of paper had fallen out of the pile he had been looking at earlier that evening and landed face-up in the middle of the room. It had just six words on it: "See the candlelit rug at midnight."

See the candlelit rug at midnight! What was that all about? Grandpa, you have some explaining to do.

Chapter 3

Ekrem couldn't sleep. He just lay awake watching the time on the alarm clock go by minute by minute. *This is worse than watching paint dry,* he thought to himself. He kept turning over and attempting to doze for a while, only to turn back over and see that only a couple of minutes had gone by. His mind went back to the message: 'See the candlelit rug at midnight'. *What was special about midnight? What did the rug do?* He desperately hoped that it wasn't an Aladdin rug that would take him somewhere else in the world. His imagination continued playing games. *Where would I want to go if it was a flying rug though? Istanbul? Another country? Greece perhaps.*

At ten minutes to midnight, Ekrem could wait no longer. He got out of bed, slid his feet into some slippers and padded off downstairs, trying not to wake his parents as he crossed over the wobbly floorboard outside their bedroom door.

It was dark in the living room. Ekrem contemplated putting some lights on but decided against it. Firstly, if his parents happened to get up and find the light on downstairs, they would probably come down to investigate. Secondly, the annoying Mehmet would probably see the light on from his house over the road and that would lead to an inquisition the next day as to what was going on. At the same time however, he didn't want to frighten Alida if she woke up and came into the room.

"Is anyone there?" he hissed as he supposedly heard footsteps approaching the living room. *A stupid question to ask,* he thought to himself, *but at least I won't scare the living daylights (or nightlights) out of someone.*

He looked out the door to check, but there was no-one there. Ekrem took down the seven candles off the mantlepiece and set them on their saucers on the seven circles of the rug – *I guess they don't have particular positions they have to go in.*

Now what? he thought to himself. "Matches, that's what I need, matches."

He crept through to the kitchen and into the bottom drawer where he found the box of long matches. He carefully tiptoed back into the living room, closed the door and struck the first match.

"Come on," he urged himself. "I need to know what happens."

After checking that all was safe, he lit all seven candles. The light of the candles brought a warm atmosphere into the room as well as casting shivering shadows across the walls that danced from the flickering flames.

"As I told you earlier," his father's voice was echoing in his head again. "The seven circles represent seven cities from the Roman Empire. All the paperwork in the files was written by your grandpa based upon his discoveries of these seven cities. As a historian, he learnt a lot – and it was his desire that you learn the same for there are great secrets that he discovered that you can only discover for yourself."

"So, what do I do now?"

He stared at the candles, but there was nothing out of the ordinary. *Perhaps I've got them in the wrong order.* He picked some up and started shuffling them around, when all of a sudden one of the candle flames suddenly shot up into an even bigger flame that Ekrem nearly fell backwards. He picked up the candle again and the flame grew shorter. *Now let's try putting it back onto that particular circle again,* he thought to himself. Once again, the flame grew larger.

"So that's how you know where to put each candle," he thought to himself.

*

By the morning everything had been put back in its place, but it didn't stop Ekrem's mother from noticing the smell in the living room. She had subsequently taken a look at the wicks of the candles and seen that they had all been lit. Now, Ekrem and Alida stood before their mother to account for what had happened.

"Now, you two," their mother started. "Someone has been lighting those candles and it wasn't your father or I. The living room smelt terrible this morning. Goodness knows what scent those candles are supposed to be. But what I want to know is which one of you two has been lighting them... Alida?"

"Not me," replied Alida putting both hands on her hips and looking at her brother with a look of 'you've-dropped-yourself-in-it-now'. "I was in my room all night."

"Ekrem?" said his mother, her voice raising in tone and sounding more infuriated.

"Do you really think I would be going about the living room lighting candles?" he bluffed.

"Yes," replied his mother. "After all it was you that the candles were left to."

Ekrem looked down at the carpet. He needed a good reason quickly. "Okay," he started, "I did light the candles in the living room. I was wide awake and couldn't sleep so I thought I would come downstairs for a while. I didn't want to put the light on in case I disturbed anyone, so I lit the candles instead."

"And why did you need to light all seven of them?" asked his mother.

"Well...," contemplated Ekrem, desperately hoping that yet another plausible reason would come into his head, which it suddenly did. "There wasn't enough light from one candle to read my book, but when I lit all seven, there was plenty of light."

His mother's eyebrow raised curiously. Ekrem's reason had certainly sounded plausible.

"I'm sorry," he said. "But no harm came about, did it?"

"No..." replied his mother slowly. "Okay, you two may go."

*

Phew! thought Ekrem to himself as they left the living room. *That was a close one.*

Alida took one look at her brother with that same suspicious look his mother had given him earlier. "You might have tricked our mother with that excuse," she started, "but you don't fool me. You didn't read a book last night. You were up to something else."

"Why do you say that?" asked Ekrem, trying to sound quite innocent.

"Because, brother, I know that you only read books on your Kindle – and in which case, you wouldn't have needed any lights on at all!"

Darn! She's clever, my sister. I shall have to be even more careful next time.

*

It was two nights later before Ekrem decided to experiment with the candles again to save any further suspicion from his parents or his sister. In the meantime, he had managed to sort out some more of the paperwork from the file and organise for definite which candle went where on the rug. Seeing this then meant he could try and solve the mystery behind the Hebrew letters.

E...S...P...T...S...P....L... it certainly doesn't seem like a word. He had even tried looking up the word in various languages including Hebrew, but the only solution he got was a word that meant 'Ask People'. *The only person I could have asked was Grandpa,* thought Ekrem to himself, *and he's dead.*

Then another thought came to him. *Perhaps it's an abbreviation. Now let's think. The 's' could be for 'secrets' and the 't' could be for 'treasure'. Hmm....*

It took Ekrem quite a long time to figure out a plausible code. "Excellent Secrets, Perfect Treasure, Surpassing Peoples' Lives". *Even so, it still doesn't make any sense.* He looked back through Grandpa's papers again, but there was still no clue.

"What are you doing?" Alida asked. "You've been sat there for nearly two hours writing something down."

"I am trying to work out what the letters stand for on the candles," Ekrem replied, still puzzled.

"Easy," said Alida. "Each Special Person Treasures Secrets Particularly Lovingly. That's what I think." She walked out of the room, looking pleased with herself.

Evil Sister Proves That She's Particularly Lousy! He didn't say it out loud. He wouldn't. He wouldn't have meant it anyway. Alida wasn't an evil sister – she was actually a really lovely sister – she just didn't understand boy things!

*

At midnight, Ekrem was back in the living room. To avoid any smell of smoke, he would open the top windows to let the air in. He carefully pulled back the curtains and quietly opened the window latches. Next, he positioned the candles back on the rug in their correct places. After this, Ekrem lit the candles, but once again, nothing seemed to happen.

"Oh, come on," hissed Ekrem, "something's meant to do something". He picked up the candle marked with the letter 'L' and to his amazement, the entire living room, the rug and the candles disappeared...

Chapter 4

Ekrem didn't know where he was. Just moments ago, he had been standing in the living room getting cross with a set of candles. Now, he seemed to be stood on a very wide stony road at the top of a high hill. On either side of him were rows of stone columns and pillars that seemed to lead towards a city not far away in the distance.

A rumbling sound came from behind him followed by the neighing of horses. He turned to see what it was. *No, it can't be, surely!* It was a horse and chariot with two men dressed in clothes that resembled that of the *Romans!*

What is going on here? How did I get here? What do I do?

"Easy," came a voice from behind him. "Follow me."

"Who are you?" Ekrem enquired, turning round to notice a boy dressed in a Roman toga stood next to him.

"Me?" answered the boy casually. "Oh, my name is Theophilus, and you are Ekrem, I suppose."

"You know my name?!" cried Ekrem. "How did you know my name?"

"Your grandfather told me," replied Theophilus.

"My grandfather!" exclaimed Ekrem. "But Grandpa only died a short while ago and you're living in the Roman era. That's nearly 2,000 years apart."

"That's right," replied Theophilus seemingly quite unphased by Ekrem's question. "Your grandfather was a lovely man – a very clever historian."

There was another rumbling sound coming from behind them. It was yet another horse and chariot and it was heading straight for Theophilus.

"Get out the way!" screamed Ekrem. "There's a chariot about to mow you down."

"I don't think so," replied Theophilus.

Ekrem closed his eyes expecting to hear a scream from Theophilus, a crunching of bones and blood splattered all over the stone road. When he did open his eyes, Theophilus was stood in exactly the same place looking perfectly normal.

"What happened?" asked Ekrem, walking around Theophilus, checking him out for any signs of injury, bruising or bleeding, but there were none.

"I just let him go through me", replied Theophilus. "Not a problem."

Ekrem's brain could not take in what was happening. *You just let a horse and chariot go THROUGH you? What kind of a person are you?* He decided that it was best not to ask and just continue with Theophilus wherever he went. There had to be a reason he was here.

"Plumbing", continued Theophilus. "That's what you are here to learn about – plumbing."

Plumbing? This wasn't one of Grandpa's secrets surely.

The two of them walked along the stone road which led closer and closer to the city. As they arrived, Ekrem couldn't help to notice the little shops on either side that were packed with customers buying colourful textiles and paying with gold Roman coins.

All around were statues of Roman gods whom the people seemed to revere. After a little while, they reached the entrance to the marketplace, known as the agora.

"Can we go in there?" asked Ekrem.

"Any reason?" replied Theophilus.

"Well," answered Ekrem, looking down at his own appearance. "I seem to be wearing pyjama shorts, a t-shirt and some flipflops. Wouldn't it be better if I was wearing Roman attire so that I look a bit more Roman?"

"Fair enough," replied Theophilus. "How much money have you got with you?"

Ekrem checked his pockets. There was nothing in them except a spare 5 kurus coin that had been sat in there for months. "This," he replied dismally.

Theophilus took a close look at the coin. "I've never seen one of those before. Is it worth much?"

"Not in my world, it doesn't," he replied. "But maybe here it does?"

Theophilus squinted and then led the way to the nearest market trader.

"I'd like this one," Ekrem said pointing to a blue toga.

"He'd like this one," Theophilus said to the market trader pointing at a white toga. He handed over Ekrem's 5 kurus coin. The market trader looked at it with a puzzled look, followed by an excited look, and then handed over the toga.

"He says he can buy two asses with that coin of yours."

Two donkeys for 5 kurus! That's surprisingly good. I should have brought more money with me.

Ekrem slipped the white toga over his pyjama shorts and t-shirt. This felt much better.

"Why did you buy me a white one and not the blue one?" he enquired.

"You need white," replied Theophilus. "Your grandfather would have wanted you to wear white."

*

By the time the sun had set, Ekrem had been on a full tour of the city, which he now knew was called Laodicea. To his amazement, he had discovered that the city was incredibly rich and had already managed to pick up no less than fifteen gold coins that people had just thrown onto the ground. Whether purposely or accidently he didn't know, but it didn't seem to matter. He tucked them into his pyjama pocket for safe keeping.

He had also seen not just one, but two amphitheatres, which totalled a seating capacity of about 40,000 people. *They must have some amazing concerts here,* thought Ekrem. He sat imagining his favourite music band playing in the open air to a Roman audience of 40,000 people. *I am not sure they would like my style of music though. Who knows?!*

It was, however, apparently dinner time and Theophilus had brought him to the house of a doctor called Lukas.

Lukas, his wife, Theophilus and Ekrem spent hours eating, drinking and discussing the city. Theophilus had been quick to introduce Ekrem as a visitor to the city who was interested in the medical work taking place there.

"Medical work," hissed Ekrem across the table to Theophilus. "What do I want to know about medical work?"

"Your grandfather would want you to know," replied Theophilus; and that was the only answer Ekrem received. Not a single word more of an explanation.

"I work for a scientific centre here," explained Lukas. "We specialise in dealing with eye ailments."

"Oh, so you're an optician then," interrupted Ekrem.

"A what?" asked Lukas. "What is an optician?"

"A person who deals with treating peoples' eyes," explained Ekrem. "They're called an optician."

Lukas seemed to ignore this piece of information and continued talking. "I produce a special salve which people put on their eyes to make them better."

"I see," said Ekrem, nodding in agreement.

"Yes, I see too," said Lukas proceeding to laugh quite hysterically.

"I didn't mean it as a joke," said Ekrem, looking rather embarrassed about what he had previously said; but both Lukas, his wife and Theophilus were finding it all very funny.

*

Mehmet looked at his clock. It was midnight and he couldn't sleep. He had already tried listening to music, reading a book, watching some videos on Youtube, but he was still wide awake. Getting out of bed, he wandered across to the window.

That's strange, he thought to himself. *There's a glowing light coming from the window of Ekrem's house opposite.* It seemed to be flickering. *It's either candles or there's a fire. Perhaps I ought to call them in case.*

But he didn't pick up his phone, instead he waited to see. It would be a little embarrassing to call the neighbours and tell them there was a fire if there wasn't one. *But what was going on? The curtains were pulled back a little and the windows were open.*

Mehmet wandered across the room, got down on his knees and pulled out the binoculars from under his bed. Once back at the window, he stared into the direction of Ekrem's living room. Sure enough, he could see candles positioned on the floor and a person stood there. It looked like Ekrem, but he couldn't be sure. Then suddenly, the person seemed to vanish as if in thin air and all the candles went out. He waited to see if the person closed the windows and pulled the curtains to, but, even after ten minutes, nothing had happened.

"I don't know what's going on over there," said Mehmet to himself, "but I'm going to find out."

*

Ekrem hadn't slept particularly well on the floor of the stone house but was awoken early by the sound of Theophilus calling in his ear.

"Time to get up, Ekrem. It's an early start at work today."

Work? Did someone say work? What work?

"We have some important plumbing to get completed. The city is dependent on everyone helping to complete the job."

"Well, can I have some breakfast first?" replied Ekrem.

"Certainly," smirked Theophilus, 'and by the time you've finished it, you will definitely want to get working."

He handed Ekrem a glass of water. "Here..."

"Is this it?"

Theophilus nodded and watched as Ekrem took the glass, took a huge gulp and then spat it all out again.

"Yuck! This water is revolting. It's warm and disgusting. Look! There's even sediments of minerals floating around in it."

"Now you see why this city needs the plumbing sorted."

"Too right I do," exclaimed Ekrem. "Now when do we get started?"

*

Chapter 5

The work was tiring and laborious. *This is worse than P.E. at school,* reflected Ekrem. *P.E. only lasts an hour, and I am normally worn out by then, but this is going on and on.* He went to look at his watch, forgetting that it was still sat on his bedside table at home.

Theophilus had seemingly left him with the workmen who were all using tools that resembled spades, pickaxes and shovels to create trenches to lay long avenues of pipe to bring water from nearby Colossae to the city. From what the workmen had managed to tell him, the water in Colossae originated in the mountains and therefore was cool, tasty and refreshing. How Ekrem wished that the work was nearly done so as to taste some of the cool water, but the trenches were a long way off complete and so no cool water could be expected today.

"So, what else can you tell me about Laodicea that would be interesting?" Ekrem enquired, thinking that conversation might help to pass the time.

"Well, about 30 years ago, in AD17, there was an earthquake here and the damage was severe. Pretty much most of the city was affected in one way or another. Some people lost their relatives and the whole city had to be rebuilt."

"Wow! Well, the Romans did a wonderful job at rebuilding it then," replied Ekrem. "Well done, Romans!" he proclaimed.

Every worker stopped their work and put down their tools. Slowly they put encircled Ekrem, looking quite aggressively at him.

"What did I do? What did I say?" said Ekrem in a panic, sensing that something bad was about to happen him.

"Would you like to say that again?" asked one of the workmen.

"Umm...no.... not really!" replied Ekrem.

"What you really meant to say was...." started another of the workmen.

"Well done, Laodiceans!" Ekrem finished the sentence, having twigged onto his mistake. "Great job, guys!" He tried to high-five them, but they had no idea what he was doing so they just stared at him. *What an idiot!*

"That's more like it," declared the first workmen. "We didn't need any help from the Romans. We rebuilt this city ourselves. We're rich here in Laodicea. That's why this is one of the banking centres of the whole Roman Empire. We don't need anyone else's help, thank you."

Incredible! It must be wonderful to be so rich that you don't need anything.

Ekrem's imagination went wandering again.

*

By the time the pipework was finished and the water from Colossae was flowing, the plan had still not worked due to the frustration of the Laodiceans. Whilst the water had left Colossae cool and refreshing, the heat of the sun on the pipes had slowly heated the water on its journey to Laodicea resulting in a lukewarm temperature that still tasted revolting.

But Theophilus came with better news to Ekrem. "Listen, Ekrem, you have worked extremely hard, so today I am going to take you to a very special place on the other side of the valley. You will certainly enjoy the water over near Hierapolis."

Theophilus and Ekrem walked for quite a few hours down the hill from Laodicea, across the valley and up the hill towards Hierapolis. Ekrem couldn't help noticing that the hills in the distance looked like they were covered in snow. *But they can't be snow. It's too warm here for snow.* Sure enough, they were covered in some sort of snow-like material that was dotted across the landscape.

"Find out about this place when you return home," said Theophilus, "and you will see what has happened in your time."

On arrival, Ekrem was impressed. There were huge pools of spring water in which the water was hot! Beautiful hot spring waters! Whilst the weather itself was hot, Ekrem couldn't wait to get in the water. Off came the clothes and straight into the pools.

"This water is amazing!" he declared, throwing the water over his neck and shoulders. "It's so therapeutic. It's better than a bath!"

Indeed, it was. This water was not going to go cold like the bath water. It even tasted good as well. All around him, people were bathing, washing, sitting and lying in the hot water. Ekrem couldn't help but notice that some of the people seemed to be unwell or disabled.

"The people here believe that the water brings healing to the body", explained Theophilus. "People come from all over the Roman Empire just to get healed in these pools."

"And do they get healed?" asked Ekrem curiously.

"Sometimes, sometimes not," replied Theophilus. "It's the same with Lukas' eye patients. Some report that they can see better, others go blind."

At that moment, a band of Roman soldiers appeared accompanied by a very elegant lady.

"Out!" demanded the Roman soldiers. Ekrem watched as the people got out the pools without question. He turned to ask Theophilus if they should leave as well, but Theophilus was already gone.

"By the name of the god Aesculapius, out!" cried the Roman soldier, pulling his whip out from behind him.

Ekrem quickly decided that this was a good moment to leave the hot spring water and run for safety, carrying his clothes under his arm. The soldiers laughed and the elegant lady got into the pool.

*

When Ekrem was sat down for dinner at Lukas' house, he shared with Lukas what had happened. Lukas once again could see the funny side of the story and was laughing quite loudly.

There was a knock at the door. Lukas went from laughing to deathly silent. He motioned for everyone to hide. He certainly wasn't expecting visitors. He slowly opened the door and a messenger boy crept in.

"What is it, Markus?" Lukas asked with a worried look on his face.

Markus stared at Ekrem suspiciously.

"Don't worry, Markus – they are with me. Why are you here?"

Markus handed over a scroll to Lukas who promptly unsealed it and read to himself the contents of the writing.

"This is from Johannes, a friend of ours. It is profoundly serious indeed. Markus, go and let the others know about this scroll. We must take note of what it says before it is too late."

He rolled up the scroll and handed it back to Markus who subsequently slipped out of the house into the night's darkness.

"Is everything okay?" asked Ekrem, noticing that the jovial Lukas he had come to know was no longer a happy man.

"That is not for you to know at this time," replied Theophilus, "but you will understand one day. Come, it is nearly time for you to leave, but before that I have gifts to give you."

Theophilus walked over to a stone cupboard built into the wall. "There are five treasures you must take from this place that your grandfather desired for you to have. You must keep them and never lose them." He handed Ekrem a small bag.

Inside the bag were four little containers, three containing liquid and one containing gold coins.

"What are the liquids?" asked Ekrem, noticing that they were all transparent and seemingly all the same.

"The first has the water from Colossae in it – it is cool and refreshing. The second has the water from Hierapolis in it – it is hot and brings healing. The third is from Lukas' own medical centre, containing an eye salve which he uses to help people see."

Ekrem admired the gold, the water and the salve. To him, they were indeed important treasures. "What about the fifth one?" he suddenly remembered.

"The fifth one is the white toga you are wearing. Remember I told you that your grandfather wanted you to wear white. Never forget it."

Ekrem nodded. Grandpa had been right. These were important treasures.

"Grandpa also mentioned about secrets in the city," Ekrem replied.

"Oh, he did, did he?" Theophilus responded. "Well, the secrets are in the treasures. I will tell you the secrets of these five, but others you will have to work out.

1. The cool water brings refreshment. The secret is that your life should be like this water and bring refreshment to other people.

2. The hot water brings healing. The secret is that when you meet people who are hurting, you can bring healing to them through the good things you do and speak.

3. The eye-salve brings sight. It is important to be able to see things with the correct perspective.

4. The gold brings wealth. Many people here in Laodicea think that gold comes from their own efforts and achievements. But the truth is that gold is a gift, and the lesson is that we must never love gifts more than the one who gives the gifts to us.

5. The white toga speaks of cleanliness. It is a reminder to keep yourself clean, not just by washing your body, but also by staying clean in your thoughts, your words and your actions.

These are the secrets behind the treasures of Laodicea."

Ekrem looked at the gifts again and then looked up at Theophilus. "Thank you," he said humbly. "Thank you for helping me understand. I will not forget my trip here."

*

Quite how Ekrem got home to his living room he did not know. The candles had somehow blown out. He quickly scrambled around to pick them up off the rug and put them back into place on the mantlepiece. Next, he closed the windows and pulled the curtains. There was one final thing to do: spray the room with the air freshener that he had hidden behind the piano. *Now no-one will know that I have been in here.*

Closing the door tightly behind him, he crept upstairs and into his bedroom, still clutching the five items that he had brought back from Laodicea. He looked at each one fondly, remembering his adventure and reflecting on the secrets that each of these treasures held.

I think I will hide them under the bed. I don't want anyone finding them yet.

*

"What was happening in your house the other night then?" asked Mehmet the following Monday.

"What do you mean?" asked Ekrem innocently.

"I mean the candles on the carpet and the lights suddenly going out," insisted Mehmet.

"Oh, that..." said Ekrem trying to stay as cool as a cucumber.

"Yes, that!" responded Mehmet. "I don't know what you're up to, Ekrem, but that definitely looked like you in that room that night – and I am going to find out what it is you are hiding. Just you wait."

No, you won't, thought Ekrem, but he couldn't be sure.

*

Chapter 6

The rug had been rolled up and put of action for the next few days much to Ekrem's annoyance. His parents, who now quite liked the idea of the rug being a permanent feature, had decided to have the living room decorated from a traditional Turkish style to that of a Roman style room. The coloured carpet, the big sofa and chairs and the multitude of pictures that covered the orange walls were going to go. Instead, the room would be painted white with marble tiling on the floor and the rug suitably positioned in the middle. The furniture would be changed into more Roman feature pieces and just a few new pictures would be placed on the wall. A couple of indoor plants, measuring about the same height as Ekrem, would be placed in giant pots at either end of the room. It seemed that the whole conversion would take about a week so. In the meantime, the rug was going to be stored in the loft.

Ekrem knew too well that the loft was too small and too crowded to unroll the rug and the thought of getting up there without waking anyone was well-nigh impossible. In addition, he wasn't entirely sure how safe it would be to light seven candles. *No, I will have to wait until the living room is complete.* In the meantime, he would continue to treasure his memories of going to Laodicea and the importance of the five items he had brought back. He had wondered about showing the water, the coins, the eye salve and the toga to his parents, but then figured that it would take quite a bit of explaining to do, so perhaps he wouldn't say anything.

"I see you are having your living room redecorated," commented Mehmet at school one day. "It probably needed doing."

"What do you mean by that?"

"Well," Mehmet started, turning to address the whole class who were waiting for the teacher to arrive to start the lesson. "The other day, our classmate Ekrem here was up at midnight burning some candles in his living room – and now they are having the living room re-done. I guess he caused a bit of an accident."

Everyone in the class laughed. Mehmet had certainly got the upper hand on Ekrem here.

"Or... his parents were so overwhelmed by the treasures that he inherited from his grandparents that they're spending it on redoing the house."

Everyone laughed again. Ekrem felt really embarrassed. He didn't know what to say. Should he reply or just let Mehmet have his moment of success? Or should he tell them a little bit about the rug?

"No, it's because the room needs to be redecorated to fit in with Grandpa's rug."

"Oh, it's Grandpa's rug that's so important, is it?" mocked Mehmet to his audience of twenty-five others. "I thought your grandfather was dead, Ekrem. He won't be bothered about what happens about the rug. Not unless you set his precious rug on fire with those candles – then he might be a bit upset – if he was alive, that is."

The twenty-five other classmates roared again and Ekrem wished that he could just evaporate into the atmosphere. Fortunately, he was saved from any more ridicule from Mehmet by the teacher walking in.

You're so irksome, Mehmet. You wait. One day you won't be making fun!

*

The living room did get completed on time and Ekrem had to admit that the room did look better. Best of all, Grandpa's rug was back in pride of place in the centre of the living room.

Good, thought Ekrem, *tonight I can light the seven candles again and see what happens.*

So, at two minutes to midnight, Ekrem climbed out of bed. He was just about to go out of his bedroom door when he heard someone in the bathroom. *Better wait until they've gone back to bed before I go downstairs.* A few minutes later, the toilet had flushed, the bathroom door had opened, the light had gone out and footsteps started padding back in the opposite direction to the stairs.

Ekrem quietly opened the door and crept downstairs and into the living room. Once again, he opened the windows, but decided to leave the curtains drawn. It wouldn't be so easy for the air to clear the smell of burning candle wax, but at least it wouldn't allow Mehmet to see anything happening.

All seven candles were placed into their correct positions. Once lit, Ekrem went over and picked up the 'L' candle again, but nothing happened. He put it down, pondering. *This is what happened last time. Why is it not working now?* He picked the candle up again, put it down again, but nothing happened. He stood there puzzled. *Was there something different about what happened last time?*

Suddenly the answer hit him. *Of course! The L candle is not going to do anything because I went to that city last time – Laodicea. I probably have to choose a different letter.*

It was at this point that he wished he had spent some time looking into the locations of the seven cities. Then he would have had a better chance to choose which place he would like to visit.

I'll go for the 'E' candle.

He stood in front of the 'E' candle. "Right, let's see if this works," he said to himself and picked up the candle.

*

Grandpa had never told anyone in his life about his own adventures to the seven cities. It had been a secret that he had taken to his grave. Not even Grandma had known. Grandpa had always considered her a bit of a gossip so had felt it best that the experiences were kept to himself.

His initial decision to give the candles, the papers and the rug to Ekrem had come when Ekrem was about seven years old. The day had been raining and it was the first time that Grandpa had decided to show the seven-year-old Ekrem some of his treasured possessions. He had taken out an ancient Egyptian signet ring which he had discovered whilst working near Thebes as a historian. The seven-year-old Ekrem had tried the ring on his finger, which was far too big for him, before sitting down with some paper and pencils and producing a picture of the ring from on the dining room table. Immediately after, his grandson had started asking him questions about the ring and then writing down the information next to the picture. *This is a historian in the making,* thought Grandpa – and this is why Grandpa had decided to leave the best item of all to Ekrem.

As for Alida, Grandpa had never really taken to her very much at all. All she ever wanted to talk about was holidays in other countries, like Florida, Paris, London and many more. When Grandpa had tried to talk to her about the history of places, Alida simply hadn't shown much interest; and as Grandpa's historical interest had never stretched further than Greece to the west and Jordan to the east, he didn't have much understanding of Western Europe or the United States of America.

"Those places don't understand our Muslim way of life," he had once said; but then after a visit to the Holy Land, Grandpa's perspective had changed for he had spent much time with Muslims, Christians and Jews whilst he was there.

When Grandma had died, Grandpa had insisted on not having her funeral at the mosque, much to the disapproval of their close friends. Instead, Grandma had been buried out at sea with family members only in attendance. There had been a few readings from the Qur'an, but also a few verses from the Torah, and another reading from the New Testament (which was from John 3:16, apparently the most famous verse in the whole Bible that talked about having everlasting life.

"That's where Grandma is now," Grandpa had said, "enjoying everlasting life."

*

As had happened before, the room and everything in it had vanished from sight. Ekrem found himself stood in front of a large building with many people walking in and out of the doors. Foolishly, Ekrem had somehow expected to arrive at the same sort of place as last time, but then his brain realised that if he was visiting different cities, then they would all look different.

"I've been here before," said Ekrem aloud to himself. "Only when I came here last time, it was in my time and the building was in ruins. This is the Celsus Library at Ephesus."

Wow! he thought to himself. *It's amazing to be in a place back in time. Just think I shall be the only person living in 2021 who has actually seen the Celsus Library in its full glory.*

Sure enough, Ekrem walked towards the entrance of the library. The building itself held about twelve thousand scrolls and was the third largest library in the whole of the Roman Empire. It had been named the Celsus Library after the Roman proconsul Tiberius Julius Celsus Polemaenus. Looking at the scrolls waiting to be read was amazing. He was just about to pick one up and unroll it when he heard a familiar voice behind him.

"You took your time getting here, didn't you?"

"Theophilus? Is that you?"

"It certainly is," Theophilus replied. "It's good to see you again, Ekrem. What's been happening?"

Ekrem proceeded to tell Theophilus about the changes to the living room and how the rug had been put away in the loft. He wasn't sure how much Theophilus would understand, but he continued talking, watching Theophilus' head nod up and down in agreement or acknowledgement.

"Come, I have much to show you here," Theophilus said, "but it's not going to be as easy here as in Laodicea. This place contains many dangers for the likes of you and I."

"More dangerous than plumbing?" asked Ekrem, half joking and half serious.

"Much more," replied Theophilus, looking very serious, stern and almost troubled.

*

As Ekrem learnt in the following hours, Ephesus was an interesting location. It was a world class centre and full of extremely intelligent people. The Romans ruled it hard and there were inscriptions to Caesar everywhere. In total, Ekrem counted twenty-five to thirty temples around the city. One of them had been erected to the goddess, Artemis, the goddess of birth and life. Her temple had one hundred and twenty-seven pillars and covered a distance bigger than one and a half football fields. Not only that, but this temple was being used as a banking centre and a place for parties.

As they walked down to the seaport, Ekrem could see the ships coming in carrying goods from all over the known Roman world. There were many different nationalities of people trading and transporting food, pottery, jewellery, spices, wine and much more. The imported goods were then being taken down to the agora (marketplace) to be sold.

"Can we go to the agora?" Ekrem asked. "I might like to buy something." He waved the 25 kurus coin that he had remembered to put in his pocket.

"Good luck getting in there," said Theophilus. "Go ahead, but I am not coming with you."

Strange, thought Ekrem. *Why wouldn't Theophilus come as well?*

He had seen some little statues of the goddess Artemis being carried by the silversmiths which would have looked quite poignant in the living room back at home. *Surely 25 kurus must be enough for one of those.*

As Ekrem walked up to one of the three gates to the agora, he was stopped by a Roman soldier blocking the way, standing by an incense burner.

"Swear your allegiance to the emperor!" declared the soldier. Ekrem watched as the person in front of him took some incense and dropped it into the burner, swearing allegiance to Caesar.

I don't have any incense. What am I going to do? I know I will try and explain and show him the 25 kurus. That will show him that I still honour leadership.

"Swear your allegiance to the emperor!" declared the soldier again.

"Well, it's like this," Ekrem started to explain, holding up the 25 kurus for the soldier to see. "I come from 2021 and we don't have Roman Emperors in our time. We have different leaders, so I was wondering..."

Ekrem didn't have time to finish his sentence. The soldier snatched the 25 kurus coin out of Ekrem's hand, looked at it and then threw it onto the floor inside the agora. Ekrem watched as some silversmiths, who had noticed the coin flying through the air, ran to get it.

"I don't have any incense..." Ekrem tried to continue.

Once again, he didn't get to finish his sentence. The soldier merely picked him up before throwing him back down on the ground. "Get out of here or I'll take you to the amphitheatre!"

Ekrem got himself up, brushed himself down, and shuffled off back to Theophilus who was stood there with his arms folded, having observed from a distance the whole thing.

"I knew you wouldn't get in there!" he said. "You can't swear allegiance to the emperor, can you?"

"Does everyone have to do that?" enquired Ekrem.

"Yes, they do or it's off to the amphitheatre."

"What happens at the amphitheatre?" Ekrem asked, looking quite perturbed.

"Simple," replied Theophilus. "The people decide if you are innocent or guilty. If you are innocent, then you are set free. If you are guilty of not showing allegiance to the emperor, then you're probably going to die. Lions!"

*

Chapter 7

As the sun started to go down, Theophilus took Ekrem to a small home on the hillside outside of the main city. It was a humble, stone building which belonged to an old lady whose husband had been taken away by the Romans years ago for not showing allegiance to the emperor.

"You'll be safe here for tonight," the old lady said. "Don't worry Theophilus, I will look after your friend."

Ekrem looked around. There was nothing much to do, not for a whole evening anyway. *What would I have done if I were at home? I probably would have been watching television or playing games. I wonder what children do here when they get bored?* He did not have to wait long to find out.

"Do you want a game of knucklebones?" the old lady asked.

"Knucklebones? What's that?"

"Surely you know how to play Knucklebones. Every Roman child knows this game."

But I'm not a Roman child, thought Ekrem. *Expecting me to know how to play Knucklebones is like expecting you, old lady, to know how to play Minecraft.* He didn't want to say anything as it might seem quite rude.

Knucklebones was a game that involved having five little bones that came from the legs of a sheep. They were small, measuring about 2.5 centimetres long. The concept of the game, Ekrem quickly learnt, was to throw the five knucklebones up in the air and then catch them on the back of your hand. According to the position they landed in, you scored different points. It was quite fun for about the first half an hour or so, but there was only so much that Ekrem could take. Firstly, he was not particularly good at catching them on the back of his hand; secondly, the old lady was winning; and thirdly there was the sound of celebration coming from down in the city.

"Ignore that music, Ekrem. Tonight is the start of the festival to Artemis for her birthday. It happens every year in the month of May. The celebrations are wild and the whole ritual is very disturbing."

Ekrem tried hard to stay focused on playing Knucklebones, but his mind kept being pulled towards the sound of the celebration. *What are they doing? It sounds much more fun than sat here playing Knucklebones with an old lady. I shall have to get out and see somehow.*

Now Ekrem knew that old people get tired easily. *If I wait long enough, she will drop off to sleep and I can slip out and see what is going on,* he thought to himself.

*

It was about two hours later before Ekrem managed to slip out of the stone house, down the hillside and into the city. There were hundreds of people everywhere. Music was playing; people were dancing; and the atmosphere was charged with excitement and enthusiasm. *Wow! This is amazing! I wish I had got down here earlier.*

Along one of the main streets there was a procession taking place. Ekrem decided to join the group of people who were all singing and dancing along. He couldn't join in the singing as he didn't know the language. *I can at least be part of the celebrations though.* The procession followed a route known as 'The Sacred Way' which eventually came to the Temple of Artemis. The people around him were taking out little statues of Artemis and dipping them into water. Ekrem was not sure why this was happening. *I shall have to ask Theophilus when I see him.*

Suddenly the atmosphere changed, and it was if the goddess Artemis had looked down from her celestial palace in the sky and brainwashed the complete town of Ephesus to go from 'partying' to 'absolute craziness'. Ekrem could hardly believe his eyes! The behaviour of the people was unthinkable, even the temple priests were involved, behaving like wild animals in the zoo. The shouting, screams and violence was so bad that Ekrem knew he had to get out of the place.

He quickly ran through a few streets towards the harbour before literally bumping into a man who had a long beard and some strange necklaces round his neck and some unusual rings on his fingers.

"Sorry..." Ekrem called out before realising that this stranger may not understand him.

"Do you believe in magic, young man?" the stranger asked.

"Well... I don't know... I've seen the occasional magic before."

"You've seen magic?" said the stranger. "Then you must come with me, and I will show you more."

Hmm... pondered Ekrem. *I'm not sure whether this is a clever idea or not.* His heart was telling him to go back to the cottage and try to forget the events of the evening, but his mind was still intrigued. *It wouldn't hurt to learn a new trick that I could show my friends at school, would it?*

"Alright then," he replied to the stranger, "lead on."

*

Had Ekrem remembered his lessons from school about 'Stranger Danger', he might have not gone with the man, but curiosity had got the better of him. As he followed the strange man, they arrived at the side of a lake. Here sat a group of people known as Oracles who normally lived in the temple. They were sat around the water, making strange chants and sounds. The stranger sat with them and joined in. Ekrem decided to stay back a few steps and watch from a distance.

"Aren't you going to show me some magic then?" asked Ekrem impatiently after about ten minutes.

"Shush!" replied the man he had followed. Ekrem waited. All of a sudden, the whole group stood up and started chanting the same words louder and louder and louder. Then they started jumping up and down, shouting and screaming. This was followed by drumbeats accompanied by the people running around crazily, rolling around on the floor, making animal noises and waving burning sticks of fire around.

This is not magic, thought Ekrem. *These people are just as crazy as the last lot. What is going on here?*

He started to leave and set off towards the harbourside which would eventually lead to the road running back up the hillside. The passers-by were still singing, dancing, shouting and playing music. He passed a food stall selling meat that had been cooked over an open fire. It smelt absolutely delicious. Ekrem stared at it, his mouth salivating, desperately wanting to have some.

The stallholder held out some meat on the end of a large fork and offered Ekrem a silver cup of a drink that looked like red wine.

"What meat is it?" Ekrem asked the stallholder. "Strangled pig," the man replied.

Yuck! I'm not eating that then however good it might smell.

"Drink?" said the stallholder, pushing the cup closer to Ekrem's lips.

"I don't drink wine," replied Ekrem. "I'm too young for that."

The man let out an enormous roar of laughter. "Wine!" he chuckled to his wife. "The boy doesn't know what this is." He turned to Ekrem. "You'll be fine with this drink, boy. It's not wine...." Ekrem smelt it. It was foul. "This is pig's blood!"

*

Ekrem's legs ran the fastest they had ever run in his life. *If I had been in the long-distance sprint race on Sports Day, I would have won easily by now,* he told himself. He arrived safely back at the stone house and let himself in. There was a sound of snoring from the far side of the room. *Good, the old lady is asleep.* He tucked himself down and slept for the rest of the night.

*

When he awoke, Theophilus had already arrived at the house. "Wake up, sleepy," said Theophilus. "I have something important to show you today – the treasure that your grandfather wanted you to come to Ephesus to receive."

Ekrem let out a great yawn. "I'm sorry," he said. "Bit of a late-night last night."

"But you went to bed very early," said the old lady. "Right after our game of Knucklebones."

Theophilus took a closer look at the black bags hanging around Ekrem's eyes. "It looks to me as if Ekrem didn't get much sleep at all."

Within an hour, they had said goodbye to the old lady and returned back into the city. Everything was quite different this morning and Ekrem was glad that some sense of normality had returned to Ephesus. As they neared the temple of Artemis, Theophilus noticed a small statue of Artemis lying on the ground. "This," he informed Ekrem, "is the main symbol of Ephesus for the Roman worshippers who live here. Do you know what they do with these statues?"

"Dip them in water?" responded Ekrem, still half awake and not thinking about what he was saying.

Theophilus stopped abruptly. He turned on Ekrem. "How did you know that? Only those attending the festival of Artemis would know that this takes place. Did you come down into the city last night? How dare you, after I tried to protect you from the terrible behaviour that takes place at this festival. Now what did you do? What did you see?"

Ekrem lowered his head and began to recall everything that had happened the night before. Theophilus' eyes grew wider and wider – not because he didn't know about the behaviour of the people, but because he couldn't believe that Ekrem had allowed himself to get involved in it all.

"I kept you at the old lady's house because it was a safe place of calm and tranquillity. Don't you realise the danger you put yourself in? I told you that this place was a dangerous place to live."

"I'm sorry, Theophilus," cried Ekrem, recognising his own stupidity as well as the disappointment in Theophilus' eyes. "Please forgive me. I will always do as you tell me in the future. I won't disobey your authority again."

Theophilus looked at him sternly and yet there was a deep look of compassion in his eyes. "I forgive you, Ekrem. I only want your best."

"Thank you..."

*

At that moment, a messenger came running around the corner. He looked hot, tired and exhausted. The sweat was running down his face and dripping onto his toga. Seeing Theophilus he ran up to him and stopped, bending over, panting for breath and wiping the sweat from his brow with the sleeve of his toga.

"Theophilus...I have been looking everywhere for you. I knew you had arrived here in Ephesus, and I assumed that you would be in the place that you normally stay with the old lady, but you weren't there." He took another deep breath. "This is an urgent message that has come to you from the island of Patmos. I have been instructed that you must read it with immediacy."

Theophilus broke the seal and unrolled the scroll. He quickly scanned the message and a sense of urgency appeared over his face. "Quick," he said. "Arrange a meeting for tonight with Timotheus and Paulus and some of the other faithful people here in Ephesus. The message in this scroll is indeed important."

The messenger took back the scroll and disappeared off as quickly as he had arrived, the dust flying off the back of his sandals.

"Is everything okay?" asked Ekrem concerningly.

"It will be," replied Theophilus. "But come, I still have something to show you."

*

A short walk further and they had arrived at the temple of Artemis. All was quiet. Theophilus led Ekrem around to a small courtyard surrounded by trees and in the centre of it all, one incredibly special tree. It looked extremely old and yet its luscious, green leaves looked young, healthy and vibrant.

"It is this tree that your grandfather wanted you to visit here in Ephesus for it holds both the secret and the treasure that you need," explained Theophilus. He picked a leaf off of the tree and handed it to Ekrem. "This is your treasure," he said. "Look after it with great care."

Ekrem looked at the leaf. It was a beautiful leaf, an unusual leaf, but at the same time it was just a leaf. "I shall," he replied. *I don't quite get what this is all about but clearly it is very significant.*

It was if Theophilus had read Ekrem's mind. "Let me tell you about the tree in this garden, Ekrem. The people of Ephesus come to this tree for hope when they need help with money or family. They think that this tree brings life, and it is therefore known as 'The Tree of Life" to the goddess Artemis. Only those who are faithful to Artemis can come into this courtyard and experience this tree for themselves.

"So, what are we doing here then?" asked Ekrem. "You know what I think about the goddess Artemis!"

Theophilus smiled. "I know, Ekrem. You don't believe in the Roman gods. Neither do I, but the secrets are this:

1. Not everyone believes the same things, but it is important to respect one another.

2. Not everything we do is right, but we can learn from our mistakes and gain forgiveness.

3. There is always hope that can be found even when everything around seems terrible.

4. For every faithful person to their true God, there is a tree waiting for them that promises them life forever.

This is what your grandfather wanted you to know."

Ekrem stood still and reflective for some moments, looking at his leaf and gazing upon the tree. *Amazing,* he thought. *What a secret and a treasure to learn from the city of Ephesus.*

"By the way, Theophilus, why do...?" But Theophilus had gone.

*

Within moments, Ephesus itself had also disappeared and Ekrem found himself stood back in his living room. The candle flames had gone out and he stumbled around in the darkness to put the candles back onto the mantlepiece. *Now I must put the air freshener around,* he thought, ensuring that the scent of candle wax would not linger in the air for too long.

There was a click as Ekrem put the top back on the can of air freshener and returned it to its hiding place. This was followed by another click, but this time from one that he hadn't expected. The living room lights had come on and a familiar voice spoke quite directly.

"What exactly has been going on here?"

*

Chapter 8

Ekrem was taken quite aback. He hadn't been expecting anyone else to be around.

"Alida! What are you doing down here?"

"No, Ekrem, let me ask you again...what have you been getting up to down here?"

"Don't talk so loudly," he hissed, "or you'll wake Mum and Dad up. What time is it anyway?"

"Ten minutes past midnight," Alida replied.

Incredible! thought Ekrem. *I have been in Ephesus for the majority of two days and yet only ten minutes has gone by here. It's like existing between two worlds and two dimensions of time.*

Ekrem went over and closed the living room door. He switched on the tall lamp in the corner of the room to give some light, but not enough to be seen through the gap underneath the door in the opposite corner. The main lights were then turned off. Alida, having noticed a leaf had been dropped on the floor, had picked it up and then gone and sat on the sofa.

"I don't recognise this leaf," she said. "There's not a plant in this room like this."

"No, I know there's not. That leaf is very important. Can I have it back please?"

Alida went to hand it to him and at the last minute pulled her hand back a little, still clutching the leaf.

"Not until you tell me what is going on here. Where did you get this leaf from anyway? Why is it so important?"

Ekrem took a deep sigh. He could see that he was going to have to explain everything to Alida, but it wasn't going to make her believe. *How do I possibly explain time-travelling, meeting people like Theophilus, and bringing back secrets and treasures from different cities?*

"It all starts with the seven circles and the seven candles," he started, and for the next thirty minutes he proceeded to tell Alida all that had happened.

"You mustn't tell anyone," he warned Alida, "not even our parents. They would stop it straight away."

"It's alright. I won't tell anyone," Alida replied. "But I would like to come next time."

"I'm not sure you should," replied Ekrem, quite concerned about the thought of his younger sister coming too. *After all, anything might happen, and I would be responsible.*

"Oh please!" said Alida. "You can't deny me an opportunity like this."

"I'll think about it..."

He's beginning to sound like our parents, Alida thought to herself. *Grown-ups say things like "I'll think about it..." That normally means it's a 'no' but they haven't yet thought of a reason why it's no.* Another thought then came into her mind.

"Well…if you do say no, I could always try it out myself I suppose…" Alida said, looking at her brother with that innocent, puppy-face look.

"No…I've thought about it, and you can come…" Ekrem replied promptly, knowing that Alida was serious and would try it out for herself – and if she did that, he couldn't guarantee what she would get up to. "I will look after you the whole time…"

Well, I hope I can. He paused. His mind suddenly downloaded another thought. *Perhaps the rug won't work for two people. After all, Grandpa did leave it to me, so maybe Alida won't be able to come after all.* He hoped she wouldn't.

*

By the time Ekrem got downstairs at two minutes to midnight the following night, Alida was already waiting for him. She had already positioned the candles into their right positions and ensured that both the matches and the air-freshener were ready to be used at the right times.

"So, what happens now?" she enquired.

"I light all seven candles and then we go and stand next to one of the letters, but not the 'L' or the 'E' because I've already been to those two cities. Besides which, I don't think they would work again anyway." He lit the candles and the two of them went and stood next to the letter 'T'. "Now I will pick up the candle and if this works correctly, we will both arrive in a different city within a few seconds."

He picked up the candle and sure enough, the living room went dark yet again, and everything disappeared.

*

In a flash of a moment, Ekrem found himself standing inside a city with a very large fortress nearby. Battalions of Roman soldiers were preparing to leave. Looking to his left and his right, he noticed that he was alone. *Good,* he thought to himself, *Alida didn't get here after all. That means I won't have to look after her and that it was only me that Grandpa meant to find out these secrets and keep the treasures.* He looked around again. There was no sign of Theophilus either. *Normally he arrives when I get somewhere. I wonder what's happened.* He then remembered about the meeting that Theophilus was going to have in Ephesus with Timotheus and Paulus and the others. *Perhaps he is really busy.* He paused, taking in the sights around him. *What am I going to do?*

"Excuse me," he said to one of the townsfolk who were walking by. "Where am I?"

"Just there," replied the man. "About three footsteps in front of me."

Ekrem was not amused, but the other man was chuckling to himself.

"That's not what I meant," replied Ekrem sarcastically. "What I wanted to know is what is this place? What is the name of the city?"

"Thyatira," replied the man. "A fantastic city – founded by Alexander the Great and the best place in the whole Roman Empire if you ask me. I mean, look around you.

There's trees, beautiful scenery, a fantastic agora, the temple to Apollo, the Roman fortress, plenty of wealth and prosperity, job opportunities galore, what more could you want?"

Hmm...sounds great. Certainly not like Laodicea or Ephesus.

"Thank you," answered Ekrem. "Have a wonderful day."

The man beckoned his hand and continued walking towards the Roman fortress. Ekrem, on the other hand, started wandering towards the agora further down the hill, which from a distance seemed to be bustling with people buying all manner of different items. He put his hand in his pocket. Yes, he had remembered to take a 50 kurus out of his piggy bank. *This should buy me something really good.* He hoped that he would be able to get in.

*

The agora at Thyatira was completely different from that of Ephesus. For a start, there were no Roman soldiers barricading the way; and there were no incense burners either. Clearly trading here was easier, and as Ekrem went into the market, he could see why.

Aside from food and drink, the main items for sale were textiles (fabrics) or silver. The textiles were exquisite, handcrafted by the people who lived here in Thyatira, mainly by women but some by men. There were beautiful togas, carpets, hats, coats and much more. Each trader was surrounded by people looking at things, picking them up before bartering for a decent price and then buying it. The most amazing part of it all however were the colours. The browns, creams, blacks were all pretty standard and usual; but the red colour was incredible. At no other time had Ekrem seen people wearing this most amazing red. Indeed, when he asked about the prices of different colours, he was staggered to discover that a red toga cost nearly three times the price of a brown one. He thought about whether he should take out his 50 kurus coin and negotiate for a red toga. That would be so impressive to show his friends at school, particularly for the next History Day. He was about to haggle with the trader when he remembered that he already had the white one from Laodicea. *Having two would be a bit of a waste. I am sure I will find something else that's exciting.*

The next trader was trading virtually the identical sorts of textiles, but deep within the pile of garments was another unusual one hidden away. This time it wasn't red, but purple – a beautiful purple that looked rich and elegant. He picked it up and slipped it over his head. Immediately all the people around him started laughing. First, the garment was too big for him that it barely stayed on his shoulders and most of it was hanging off of him like some gigantic nightdress from his great-grandmother's wardrobe. Second, the trader called out "that one's for women" which kept everyone reeling in laughter.

"I'm trying it on for my mother," joked Ekrem, trying to get himself out of the small, ridiculing crowd that surrounded him. He quickly gave it back to the trader who rearranged it neatly on her table.

"See that, Lydia, a boy with some spunk about him."

"Spunk?" thought Ekrem. *I'm not familiar with that word, but I'll look it up when I get home.*

He promptly left that particular part of the agora and wandered around to look at some items that weren't textiles. He eventually found the silversmith and spent time admiring the items that were being hammered out to form bowls, utensils and even weapons!

"Don't you touch anything, young man," bellowed a rather short, tubby trader with a large hammer in his hand. "Most of this stuff is reserved for the Roman fortress up there and they won't want young boy's fingerprints on there too."

Ekrem nodded in agreement. He was still desperate however to spend his 50 kurus. "I have some silver," he called out to the trader. "I can give it to you, and you can give me something else – a swap, for example." He held out the coin and the trader put down his hammer and came wandering across to have a look at it. He took the coin out of Ekrem's hand and had a close look at it before returning it back to him. "Look, young man, there's things that are silver and things that look like silver but aren't silver. What you have there... looks like silver but is really copper and nickel which means it is no good to me."

Ekrem looked down at his coin with disappointment.

"It's an important lesson to learn," the man continued. "What looks good might not always be good. Remember that!"

"Here, here!" said another voice from behind Ekrem. It was a voice he recognised.

"Theophilus! You made it!"

"Indeed, I did, but I can't stay long, Ekrem. The secrets and treasures of Thyatira you are going to mainly have to search out for yourself. I have however been asked to find a lady called Lydia to look after you whilst you are here, but I don't know what she looks like, but apparently most people know her."

"I think I've already met her," replied Ekrem. "Come on Theophilus, she sells the most amazing purple toga that would be great for your mother..."

*

It was a few hours later that Ekrem was in Lydia's house trying to help her complete some cooking of something that resembled something like cheese balls mixed with flour, known as popona. These, as Lydia explained, were to be made as an offering to the god Apollo. There had to be nine balls accompanied by laurel leaves. Ekrem stood counting the balls, realising that there were more than nine.

"There's eighteen balls here, Lydia," he informed her politely.

"Yes," Lydia replied. "Jezzy, from the textiles guild, will be popping by to collect them shortly. I said that I would bake nine for her to take to the temple of Apollo this evening. Get a container of laurel leaves ready for me, will you, Ekrem?"

Ekrem looked across at the container and the laurel leaves lying on the table. "Sure," he said. He organised the leaves into the container and Lydia brought across the food to put on top of them. As she did so, there was a knock on the door and Ekrem went to answer it.

"Is Lydia there?" asked a young lady. "May I come in?"

"Come in Jezzy," came Lydia's voice from the other side of the room.

Jezzy walked in, hugged Lydia and then sprawled herself across the Roman lexus (couch). "Isn't life good?" she said. "It's been a good day trading in the agora and tonight is the initiation of the guilds at the Temple of Apollo. I can't wait. It's so exciting."

Lydia reluctantly nodded but didn't reply. Jezzy's attention turned to Ekrem. "Aren't you a fine, young man? Now, let me see, give a minute and...." She stopped mid-conversation. Ekrem wasn't quite sure what he was waiting for, but then Jezzy spoke again. "You're a visitor here to Thyatira, aren't you? You are going to find yourself with a decision to make whilst you are here. The right decision might not always be what it seems. You will discover some treasure here in Thyatira and then you will take it home with you and share it with a girl similar to you, but a little younger. She will also have something to tell you and you will both be amazed but beware because this girl is also not to be trusted."

Ekrem's mind did not know what to think. Some of what Jezzy said seemed to be absolutely true. Yes, he was a visitor here. Yes, he would find a treasure because that's what he was here to do. Yes, he would go home and show a girl younger than him – that would be his sister, Alida; but the last part didn't seem to make much sense. *My sister is not to be trusted? I can't believe that. Alida is so good, so faithful, so kind...*

"How do you know all this?" Ekrem swung around to face Jezzy and confront her, partly out of curiosity and partly to defend the honour of his sister if he needed to.

Jezzy didn't get time to answer because Lydia did it for her. "She's a prophetess, Ekrem. She helps us to understand our culture and our religion. She's extremely intelligent and has learned a lot from the Roman schools of thought."

At that moment, a bee flew through the open window and into the room. Jezzy got off the couch and started running around the room, waving her arms and shouting.

"Don't worry, I'll get it. It won't sting you," cried Ekrem, chasing after the bee.

"I'm not scared, Ekrem! It's a messenger from the gods to bring good news. Oh, this is wonderful!"

Ekrem looked at her strangely. *It's just a bee!*

*

Chapter 9

"What time are you going to the temple tonight, Lydia?" Ekrem asked inquisitively, noticing that the sun had already gone down; and judging by the noise of the people passing the door, most people had already set off for the temple.

"I'm not going," replied Lydia. "I can't, Ekrem. I don't believe in Apollo. I have a different faith. Here in the city of Thyatira, they believe in Apollo being the sun god who brings life to everything around. I believe in a different god, and he bears no resemblance to Apollo whatsoever. The God I believe in has brought life to me in a different way."

"Well, that's alright. People are allowed to have differences of belief and opinion," Ekrem replied in a matter-of-fact voice.

"Not here in Thyatira, Ekrem," replied Lydia in both an upset and an annoyed tone. "You don't understand the difficulty with the decision I have had to make to not go tonight. From tomorrow, everything will change for me. You'll see, but somehow it'll be okay."

Ekrem didn't know what to say. He sat just staring at the night sky. Far in the distance was a solitary, bright and beautiful star – a gem on a velvet cover.

*

Lydia and Ekrem were awoken early the next morning by a loud knocking on the door. Outside stood Jezzy looking quite flustered.

"Lydia, Lydia, where were you last night? You weren't at the temple. What happened?"

"I didn't come, Jezzy. I knew that I couldn't."

"What do you mean?! You've got to be there. You know what's going to happen if they realise you weren't there. Now I am prepared to say that you were there and account for you as a witness, but you will need to take your offering to the temple right now and leave it there with the others before the priests clear them away."

"I'm not doing it, Jezzy. I know the risk I am taking."

Ekrem, who had been witnessing the conversation from a distance, could hold back no longer. "I don't know what is going on, but I am sure there is an easy solution (at least that's what my dad always says when my mum is going on about something). Just tell me what the problem is."

Lydia and Jezzy both took a deep sigh and began to explain to Ekrem the situation. It seemed that in the city of Thyatira every craftsman, blacksmith, silversmith, potter, baker, tanner, etc. had membership to belong to a guild or society. These guilds meant that you could trade your goods in the city, but without the membership, you could no longer trade. Memberships were renewed at a festival held at the temple of Apollo where the person would offer Apollo a gift and give recognition to the god as lord. Lydia was supposed to have gone to the temple, but she hadn't – and now Jezzy was trying to save the situation.

"I know what you're thinking, Lydia," continued Jezzy. "You're wanting to stick close to the religion that both you and I belong to, but you need to do what I did.

Listen, you have to think logically. You have to think carefully about your livelihood and survival. Don't worry about going to the temple of Apollo. Quickly, go now and leave the sacrifice and then I will vouch for you. You will be able to continue life as normal and no-one will worry about you."

"What happens if you don't go?" enquired Ekrem. "Will you die?"

"No," replied Lydia, "but I won't be able to trade in the agora. Without trading, I will have no money, no job and that could mean no home either."

"So, why don't you just go and do what Jezzy says now? If I had known all this last night, I would have taken you down there myself – or even done it for you."

Lydia smiled sweetly at him. "That's kind of you, Ekrem. But I won't do it and I won't let you do it either."

Jezzy threw her head back, her hands in the air, and let out a deep sigh of frustration. "I can't believe you are doing this, Lydia. Just a simple compromise would do to keep your life straightforward here in Thyatira. Don't you value your job? Don't you value the money? Or is your rebellion to the Roman gods more important?"

Lydia didn't reply. Jezzy walked across the room and straight out the door.

*

"What will you do now?" Ekrem asked Lydia.

"I will take my textiles and leave here very quickly. There will be no place for me here. My last amount of money will take me by boat across the sea to Macedonia. I will try and find a place to join people like myself and trade my textiles there. Somewhere like Philippi, I guess."

"Can I give you something before you go?" asked Ekrem, feeling in his pocket for the 50 kurus coin. "I don't know if it will be of any use to you, but I want to give it to you." He held out the silver coin.

Lydia took it and looked at both sides. "Who's this?" she asked, looking at the man's head on one side.

"Kemal Ataturk", he replied. "But don't ask any more questions, it's too complicated to explain."

"I have something for you too, Ekrem." Lydia went over to the couch and reached for something that was hidden underneath it. She brought out a necklace and on it was a silver star. "One of the silversmiths made it for me," she said, "but I want you to take it."

"It's absolutely gorgeous," said Ekrem, turning the necklace over and over in his hand, admiring its beauty and glint of the shimmering silver. "It reminds me of that star I saw last night. But why do you want me to have it?"

"It is a bright and morning star. It will remind you of this time in Thyatira and of me, Lydia. Maybe one day you will learn more from your visit here as well."

*

Saying goodbye to Lydia was not the easiest thing Ekrem had ever went to do. *In a sense Lydia is becoming a bit like a refugee,* he thought to himself.

Leaving a country and going to another to try and start life all over again. I will try and think differently about refugees from now on.

Having left Lydia's house, Ekrem went back to the place where he had first arrived at Thyatira – a beautiful location where he could look across the landscape at the beautiful city below. It was as he arrived that Theophilus also appeared.

"I am sorry I couldn't be with you until now. Has everything been okay? I got held up by a messenger that had an important message to deliver to me and a few other people here in Thyatira. Have you discovered the secret or treasure yet?" Theophilus enquired.

Ekrem looked at him with a half-smile on his face and half-sadness in his eyes. "I have discovered both," he said, showing Theophilus the beautiful silver star necklace that Lydia had given him. "This is the treasure for sure."

"And the secrets?"

"I have learnt a few," responded Ekrem. "Secrets I shall never forget.

1. Things are not always what they seem even if they look like it.

2. Compromise is easy, but it isn't always right.

3. How much do I value the things around me?

4. Will I let my circumstances tell me what to do, or will I do what I believe I should even if it means losing out on other things?

"Wow! That's deep thoughts, Ekrem," said Theophilus, looking quite astounded.

"Well, I did have some help from Lydia," he replied. "I am not sure about Jezzy though. She seemed to have some rather unusual ideas, including something about not trusting my sister."

"Don't listen to her, Ekrem. Your sister is a very trustworthy person."

"But you've never met her," replied Ekrem. "So how would you know?"

"I may not have met her yet," started Theophilus, "but I know someone called Kayra who has."

Kayra? wondered Ekrem. *Who is Kayra?*

*

Chapter 10

When Ekrem had picked up the candle, Alida also found herself encountering a new experience. The living room had disappeared, and she found herself standing in a small, rectangular plot of land surrounded by a fence. All over the ground were large stones, broken stone pillars and ancient foundations. These were separated by trees that had grown up all around, providing much needed shade from the summer sun. This place had obviously been quite a significant site in history, but now it was a pile of stones. Outside the fence, cars and traffic were whizzing by, tooting horns. Cyclists were weaving their way in and out of traffic. The shops and buildings on the opposite side of the room were busy with customers buying all sorts of goods from mobile phones to jewellery, food to tourist souvenirs.

Alida looked around. There was no-one else in this garden of ruins. *Ekrem didn't come,* she thought, with disappointment that this was not going to be an adventure they were going to have together. She imagined him still stood in the living room, expressing irritation that she had disappeared, and he was still stood there.

What doesn't make sense is that Ekrem always talked about going back to the Roman times and this place is certainly not in history. This is the here and now. How am I going to find any great secret or treasure here?

She imagined returning to the living room empty-handed and trying to explain to Ekrem how she hadn't gone back in time at all, and how there were no secrets and treasures to be found in what seemed to be just a normal, busy Turkish town or city. She wasn't sure which town though. She only knew that she had never been in this place before, wherever it was. Her thoughts suddenly became interrupted.

"Oi, you, have you got any money to spare?"

Alida turned around to see four boys of about her age standing on the opposite side of the mesh fence. They looked mischievous and over-confident.

"No, sorry, I don't," Alida called back. The boys looked disappointed and muttered between one another. Alida had expected them to move on and find someone else to ask for money, but they stayed at the fence just watching her. It was most intimidating and disconcerting.

"What are you doing anyway?" one of the boys called out to her.

What am I doing? I don't even know what I'm doing, or why I'm here or anything.

"Just looking at these stones," Alida replied, hoping that a boring answer would send the boys away.

"My name's Bulad," yelled one of the boys, "and these are my friends. We could keep you company if you're feeling a bit lonely." The other boys laughed a little.

Alida had no intention of going with the boys at all, but at the same time she did not want to appear impolite. She started to walk towards the fence.

"Don't go with them," came a different voice from behind her. Alida swung around, oblivious to the fact that someone else had come into the ruined garden. Stood a few metres away from her was a girl with long, brown hair. She was stood with her hands on her hips and looked like she was extremely confident. *She almost looks powerful,* thought Alida. *There's something unusual about this girl. There's a sense of warmth, care and concern radiating off of her.*

"Who are you?" asked Alida, trying to make sense of the fact that people just seemed to be talking to her and around about her unexpectedly.

"My name is Kayra," the girl replied. "I am here to help you, Alida."

"You know my name?!" Alida exclaimed. "I mean, how?"

"I told you, I've been sent to help you during your time here in Akhisar. It's important that you understand what you are seeing."

Akhisar! Alida thought. *So that's where I am.* Her mind quickly flashbacked to another time when she had been much younger, and her parents had brought her to this city to visit some friends that they knew; but she had never been in this part of the city before. She looked around again. The four boys were still watching from the fence.

It just doesn't make any sense. I am stood surrounded by bits of old boulder, stone, pillars and I am supposed to understand what I'm seeing.

Kayra had read her mind. "Listen, Alida. Let me get you started. You got here because of a rug that your grandfather left your brother. Is that right?"

Alida nodded. *I have no idea how she knows all this information, but I will let her continue for the moment.*

"Your brother has been going back in time and finding out secrets and treasures from the different places he's been visiting, yes?"

Alida nodded again. *How does she know all this?*

"And you are wondering why you are here?"

Obviously! thought Alida sarcastically.

"Alida, your brother is being helped by a friend of mine called Theophilus. He is helping Ekrem to discover the secrets and treasures of these places from times past. But your interest was never history. Your interest is geography and that's why you're here in the present here-and-now. This is exactly the same location as your brother would be in, but in present day, not back in time."

"You mean, he's in exactly the same area but back about 2,000 years ago; and I'm seeing the same place in 2021," Alida clarified.

"Exactly!" responded Kayra. "Now can you imagine how amazing it will be when you and your brother start to talk about what you've both seen?"

I certainly can, pondered Alida. *It will be fun to talk about how a place was and what it has now become.* Her brain suddenly interrupted her train of thought.

"Hang on a minute, Kayra. What is it about here that is supposed to be so interesting? It's just a pile of broken pillars, boulders, stones and trees, isn't it?"

*

"Who are you talking to?" came Bulad's voice again. He and his three friends had come into the garden and were heading towards Alida.

"Kayra, this girl here," Alida replied.

The boys looked confused. Kayra put her finger to her lip. "They can't see me," she whispered to Alida. "Just continue as normal. I will sort them out if they start to be a nuisance."

"She's gone mad, boys," said Bulad to his mates. "There's no-one else here. The girl has gone insane." The boys laughed again. "Clearly, pretty girl, you are a stranger around here and you're lost. Perhaps your parents have wandered off into one of the shops or something and you're stuck here by yourself. So, whilst you're waiting, why don't you spend some time with us, eh? We will look after you. Not everyone around here, can be trusted, can they boys?"

The other boys all smirked and giggled amongst themselves. "Certainly not us lot anyway", the tall, skinny one said. By now the boys had made a circle around Alida. She looked across at Kayra with a desperate look for help.

"Okay, now the fun begins," said Kayra. She marched straight up to Bulad, grabbed him by the back of his t-shirt and pulled him backwards and down onto the ground. The other boys took a step back.

"What happened?" they asked Bulad.

"I don't know," said Bulad, shocked and bewildered at how he had suddenly found himself lying flat on his back by the side of a tree root.

Alida looked across at Kayra who smiled back with a cheeky grin. Kayra ran across, grabbed the next boy, and pulled him back onto the floor, then the next one and then the last one. All four boys were on the ground whilst Alida had stood there just watching.

"How did she do that?" asked one of the boys, brushing himself down and trying to get back up again. No sooner had he got up then Kayra pushed him back down again.

"Just to make the point," Kayra said justifying herself to Alida for pushing the boy down again. "These boys need to learn to treat girls like ladies!"

The four boys eventually got themselves to their feet. "Quick," cried Bulad. "Let's get out of here before she does anything else to us!" He and the other three boys went skidding off across the stones and grass until they were well out of sight.

"Thanks, Kayra!" said Alida.

"I told you I'm here to look after you," said Kayra. "Now let's get down to business."

*

A small mini coach pulled up on the side of the road and some tourists clambered off the vehicle, looking slightly stiff and relieved to be back in the fresh air. Most of them looked very English and predominantly in their fifties or sixties. One man, who was probably in his thirties, was looking around quite frantically before taking off, leaving the others behind, and disappearing into the nearest public convenience. He re-joined the group a short while later, looking and feeling most relieved.

Alida had expected the group to go wandering off to the shops and cafes as normal tourist groups do when they disembark from a coach in a new city. This group however was different. They came into the same plot of land that Alida and Kayra were stood in. They too were wandering around the site examining the old stones, the broken pillars and the trees. Most of them had their cameras or mobile phones out and were taking pictures of the ruins around them.

"What are they doing taking photos of this place, Kayra?" asked Alida. "It's not the kind of thing you normally would take holiday photos of." She thought about her own album at home that had photographs of beaches, swimming pools, restaurants, dolphins, animals and much more. She herself had never taken any photographs of just some old broken stones. "Are they archaeologists?"

"No," replied Kayra. "They're tourists on holiday."

"So, what's so important about this place?" Alida asked. "There has to be a reason."

"There is, Alida, and most of it will make more sense when you start to talk with your brother Ekrem about what he has seen. But for the moment, you need to remember this: this site was once a particularly important one, a place where a particular group of people would come together as a community to care for one another and support one another despite opposition from the Romans. They kept faithful to what they believed and were on an upward trajectory. However, they were warned that if certain things didn't change, then their community would come to nothing. Look around you, Alida, this is what is left – broken stones, pillars and boulders that speak of what was once a thriving community but is no longer."

"But what about all the city around it?" protested Alida. "The shops, the businesses, the traffic, everything here is thriving!"

"True," replied Kayra, nodding her head in agreement. "But it's the heritage of what this small place could have left behind that is now lost."

The noise of the call to prayer came resounding out across the city from the various minarets attached to the mosques. Alida watched as people entered into the mosques for their third time of prayer for the day. Others took out their prayer mats on the street (all facing in the direction of Mecca in Saudi Arabia) and started to pray.

"Kayra..." Alida started, turning back around to face her; but Kayra was gone. Once again, she was alone except for the few remaining tourists taking their last few photos. She watched as they clambered back onto the mini-coach and set off for another destination.

Funny, she thought to herself. *A group of tourists visiting an old pile of stones and pillars for their holidays. I bet that really 'ruined' their holiday!*

She sat down on one of the boulders and thought carefully. *What have I learnt from this trip to this part of Akhisar?*

1. You have to be careful who you spend time with – check that they are genuine friends.

2. Be part of a loving and caring community.

3. Some things are lost forever except for the broken stones and pillars which tell us about people and times in the past.

4. Things around may be thriving, but don't miss the legacy that history leaves for us to learn from.

5. When warnings come, take notice of them before it's too late.

*

Within seconds, Alida found herself back in the living room of their house. Ekrem was stood on the other side of the rug holding a necklace in his hand.

"I'm so sorry you couldn't come," they both said in unison, before looking at each other strangely. *What is going on? What has happened to us?* "But you weren't there," they both said again in unison.

*

It took ages for Ekrem and Alida to share about what had happened, particularly when they discovered that they had been in the same location in two different time periods.

"It's called Thyatira," said Ekrem, "and this necklace reminds me of the bright and morning star that I saw in the night sky."

"Now-a-days it is part of Akhisar – and it is really busy with traffic and tourists, businesses and cafes – and really irritating boys!"

"Yes... but the lessons we've learnt from the communities we have been in have been much greater than that, haven't they, Alida?"

"You're right, Ekrem. They certainly have."

"By the way," interjected Ekrem, looking at his sister quite intently. "Who's Kayra?"

"Ah, now she is an interesting person. You don't want to mess with her!" she laughed.

*

Chapter 11

The next morning, Ekrem and Alida's parents couldn't help noticing how tired their two children were looking at the breakfast table.

"You two look like you had a really rough night's sleep," said their mother. "It's going to be an early night for you both tonight."

Ekrem looked across the table at his sister and winked. "Better for them not to know," he whispered across the table, receiving a thumbs up in return. It did however start to make Ekrem think of how to deal with this problem. Concentrating at school had become a lot harder, partly because of the tiredness and partly because his mind kept concentrating on the experiences he had been having in the different Roman cities. *Perhaps, the rug would work at an earlier time. Mum and Dad normally go off to bed at about 10:15pm so if I went down at 11pm, I'd be back by 11:10pm and then I would get another hour's sleep. It might be worth a try.*

*

When Ekrem did arrive at school later that morning, his English teacher announced that they would be revising the use of futuristic tense. She wanted them to start with an activity in which they had to sort out nine statements about things they might be looking forward to in order of personal preference or priority. Ekrem was sat with his friend, Peroz, who seemed far more enthusiastic about the task than he was. The statements read:

* Doing well in my exams

* Scoring a goal in sport

* Getting married

* Going to a friend's house

* Having lots of money

* Working at a job I enjoy

* Having a party

* Visiting other places in the world

* Making new friends

"Well, what do you think?" asked Peroz politely, but enthusiastically.

"Peroz, I am too tired to do this. Put them in whatever order you like."

Peroz looked a little disappointed with Ekrem's response, but then happily spent a few minutes contemplating his thoughts and organising the statements into order of priority. His top choice was 'Having a party'. *Hmm...* thought Ekrem. *That just about says it all.*

After a few minutes, the teacher asked for feedback from the class. Narin explained that her top choice was 'Making new friends' because she felt that you could never know enough people, that they made her feel happy, and that friends are there for life. *Sometimes,* thought Ekrem, *but not always!*

Next Hamza went on to explain that his top choice was 'Working at a job I enjoy.' He went on to explain his aspiration to become a fighter pilot and how the particular jet he wanted to fly could deal with the aerodynamics, etc., etc., etc... Ekrem was dropping off to sleep by now.

Mehmet went next. His top priority for the future was 'Going to a friend's house'. *Weird,* responded Ekrem in his mind, *I thought he would have wanted to have lots of money or something.*

"And whose house, may I ask, are you looking forward to going to, Mehmet? You don't have to tell us, of course."

"No, it's fine," Mehmet replied, "I'm looking forward to going to Ekrem's house." *No chance,* thought Ekrem. "Apparently, he's got some really interesting things over there which I can't wait to see. In fact, I'm not just going over to visit, I'm going for a sleepover."

Ekrem was starting to wake up pretty quickly. "No, you're not, Mehmet. Stop fooling around. You're not coming to my house for a sleepover." Turning to the teacher, Ekrem said "He's joking, miss, he's only saying it to wind me up."

"No, it's true," Mehmet continued. "I'm going there tonight. My parents are going away on business for the night so Ekrem's parents said I could stay with him. It's going to be great!"

*

Ekrem could not concentrate on anything else for the rest of the lesson or for the rest of the day for that matter. *Mehmet coming round to stay. No! What a disaster! It couldn't be true, could it?*

"Mum!" he yelled as he flew open the back door that afternoon. "Did you say Mehmet could stay here tonight? Please say you didn't. He thinks he's coming over tonight…"

His mother looked him. "Calm down, Ekrem. Yes, I did say he could…." She didn't even get to finish her sentence.

"Oh Mum!" Ekrem said frustratingly. "That was just the worse idea ever! You know what an annoying, little, irksome, idiotic snob he is. I shall never live this down."

He stormed out of the room and up the stairs to the sanctuary of his own bedroom, only to find an extra bed had been placed there. *He's staying in my room! That's even worse!*

*

Mehmet arrived at about 7pm with a simple rucksack of things he would need for the night. *I hope he doesn't snore,* thought Ekrem, *that would just about be the limit.*

"Come in Mehmet," Ekrem's mother said, "Ekrem will be with you in a minute."

Ekrem came down the stairs. "Hi," he said in a matter-of-fact tone. "Bedroom is nearest the stairs, toilet at the end of the landing, living room just next to you, is there anything else you want to know?"

Ekrem's mother looked highly displeased with Ekrem's attitude. "Yes," Mehmet replied with great enthusiasm,

"Where do we start? I can't wait to see all the amazing treasures you've got!"

"Treasures?" Ekrem's mother asked curiously, one eyebrow raised at her son.

*

The evening wasn't as bad as Ekrem had expected. His father had suggested they sat down and played Trivial Pursuits, a general knowledge game that Mehmet particularly enjoyed – and won. This was followed by a drink of Turkish tea for everyone and then an episode of a comedy programme on the television. Ekrem and Alida had never seen the programme before, but Mehmet most certainly had and so proceeded to fill them all in on the plotline so far. The time by now was 9:30pm and so Ekrem's father started hustling them off to bed.

Hopefully, thought Ekrem, *Mehmet will drop off to sleep quite quickly and once I know he is sound asleep I will go downstairs and onto the next city. I will be back within ten minutes and hopefully Mehmet won't wake up. Even if he does, he should think that I've just gone to the bathroom.*

Little did Ekrem know but Mehmet had a plan too. He had observed Ekrem coming down into the living room at midnight and had worked out that there was clearly an important reason. This was his one and only opportunity to find out exactly what Ekrem was up to. He set the alarm on his watch to three minutes past midnight. Even if he did fall asleep, his alarm would wake him up and by then Ekrem would already be down in the living room. He wouldn't confront him, just merely watch what was going on.

Alida, on the other hand, had no idea of any of this. She naturally assumed that because Mehmet was staying the night, her older brother wouldn't chance going down to the living room that night. She drifted off into a deep sleep.

*

Ekrem had forced himself to stay awake. His mind and body felt exhausted, but he just couldn't miss another adventure. Two minutes to midnight eventually came. He looked over at Mehmet who was fast asleep and snoring like a hog. *Good! He won't be waking up any time soon.* He slipped out of the covers and crept across the room and then opened the bedroom door as quietly as he could. Looking left and right to check that all was clear, he made his way downstairs and into the living room. He pushed the door ajar and started to arrange the candles on their small saucers on the seven circles of the rug. It took a little while to locate the matches as his father had moved them to inside the mantlepiece cupboard. He lit the candles and went and stood next to the letter 'P'. How oblivious he was to the fact that Mehmet's face was watching him through the gap in the door from out in the hallway. Ekrem picked up the candle and the room went dark.

*

Within a flash of a second, Ekrem found himself stood in the boiling summer sun in the middle of a vineyard where both men and women were busily picking grapes for harvesting. All around him were rows and rows of vines, people with baskets and knives, and heaps upon heaps of grapes. Ekrem couldn't resist. He pulled on one of the bunches and took half a dozen grapes off in his hand before consuming them one at a time quite quickly.

"Stop there! What are you doing?" shouted a rather tall, aggressive looking man with a knife in his hand. "You know that you can't just help yourselves to grapes."

"I'm sure the owner of the vineyard wouldn't mind too much if I just had a few samples," replied Ekrem, trying to give a reasonable explanation. Clearly, he had been caught eating them, but he didn't want anything to happen to him, not having just arrived.

"I think he would mind," replied the man, who by now was right in front of Ekrem and holding the point of the knife towards Ekrem's face. "I am the owner of this vineyard and those grapes you're eating are my property."

Ekrem took a big gulp. "I'm sorry," he spluttered out. "I didn't know. I've only just arrived here. Please forgive me."

"You can't just help yourself to other peoples' belongings," said the man. "Didn't anyone ever teach you that? It's called stealing and that is breaking the eighth commandment of the Torah."

"The eighth commandment of the... what?" Ekrem replied.

"The Torah!" replied the man. "Don't you know anything about our ways here in Philadelphia?"

"I'm afraid I don't," replied Ekrem.

"Right," answered the man, "then someone's going to have to start teaching you and I guess that's going to have to be me." He lowered his knife. "My name's Rabah and these are my vineyards. The people working here are all part of the small community here. Every one of them is Jewish and we believe in our holy scriptures, the Torah. In that Torah there are ten commandments and the eighth one says, 'You shall not steal'. Do you understand?"

Ekrem nodded. This was the first time he had ever come across a Jewish community. He had heard about Jewish people but knew extraordinarily little about them. *This will be interesting,* he thought. "So, what else can you teach me?" asked Ekrem, keen to know more.

"How to get a good day's work done," demanded the man. "Pick up that knife there and start harvesting some grapes. Do it well and we'll talk later." He was about to walk off but remembered one last point. "And don't forget, no eating the grapes! No stealing!"

Crumbs! thought Ekrem. *I was tired before I got here and now, I've got to work!*

*

The views across Philadelphia were quite stunning. From the hillside where the vines were growing, you could see right across the valley and onto the hills in the far distance. The palm trees were swaying in the summer breeze and all around the vineyard were large stone pillars thar were inscribed with some writing that Ekrem didn't recognise. He later learnt that the letters were Hebrew and acknowledged the God of Abraham, Isaac and Jacob as being the one true God to the Jewish people. Across the way, there was another stone building. It resembled that of a mosque, but it didn't have a minaret or a crescent on the top. Instead, it had the symbol of a seven branched candlestick. *Interesting,* contemplated Ekrem, *it's seven candles that Grandpa left me. I wonder if there is any significance,* but he couldn't work out any. *Maybe it's just coincidence.* It turned out that this building was a Jewish place of worship known as a synagogue.

When Rabah returned later that afternoon, Ekrem had managed to harvest two buckets full to the brim of grapes. Rabah looked at him. "You're a good worker," he said.

"Thank you," said Ekrem, "can I finish now?"

"You have had enough of harvesting grapes?" Rabah answered. Ekrem nodded. "Well, I can give you an easier job to do if you like. After all, you aren't getting paid to do this work for me. Follow me."

He led Ekrem towards the courtyard near his house. In the centre of the courtyard was a big circular stone area that looked like the base of a rather large fountain or a paddling pool. In this circle, piles of washed grapes had been placed. *He's going to allow me to eat some,* thought Ekrem to himself. How wrong he was.

"Right, you can start making the wine, Ekrem. Take off your shoes. You will need bare feet for this."

"Why? What am I going to be doing?" asked Ekrem curiously.

"Treading grapes!" replied Rabah with a big smile on his face. "Dancing on them. Squeezing them. Squashing them. Whatever phrase you want to say for it, but all the juice of these grapes has got to get down the hole that's underneath them all."

"But that's going to take ages," protested Ekrem, looking at all the grapes.

"Then you'd better start dancing quickly," replied Rahab laughing, rubbing his hands with glee before walking into his house.

"Oh, Theophilus, are you there?" asked Ekrem aloud to seemingly himself. "I need your help!"

*

Chapter 12

Theophilus had not appeared that day, that evening or throughout the night. Rabah had seemingly forgotten all about Ekrem and so Ekrem spent the night lying under the vines within the vineyard. It had been a mainly undisturbed night apart from on one occasion when there had been a strange wailing noise. At first Ekrem had thought it was a dog crying, but on investigation found out that there were little foxes, known as pups, going through the vines, gnawing at the trunks, digging holes around the vines and exposing the roots and ruining the entire harvest of grapes altogether. Ekrem spent about an hour chasing these foxes away before getting some further sleep.

*

Rabah appeared about 9am the next morning. "Ah, Ekrem, shalom," he said. "I did not realise that you were still here. Did you have a good night's sleep?"

"Under a vine tree?" Ekrem asked slightly grumpily.

"Oh dear, me, what terrible hospitality I have offered you. You must forgive me. I did not think. Tonight, you will sleep in the best room in the house." He held out his hand to Ekrem as a gesture of goodwill and promise. Ekrem returned with a handshake, but no real heart feeling behind it. "Now you have some questions you wanted to ask me, no?"

Ekrem hadn't really thought of any questions. His back ached from sleeping rough all night and his mind was still merely focused on the foxes. *They're a bit like the problems we face. They can creep in when we're not expecting them, and then we have to deal with the destruction that they create. A bit like Mehmet,* he thought to himself.

"Let me tell you then about our life here," started Rabah. "As I told you yesterday, we are a Jewish community who believe in one God – the God of Abraham, Isaac and Jacob." Ekrem listened as Rabah went onto talk for about the next forty-five minutes. "The important thing here in Philadelphia however is that we do not have to pay homage to Caesar. Every other person in this city has to recognise the lordship of Caesar, but we, Jewish people, are exempt."

"That is so different from the other places I have visited so far," replied Ekrem, surprised at the favour the Jewish community was having in this city. "Why is that?"

"There's a couple of simple reasons. First, the grapes. We have the best grapes in the whole of the Roman Empire. Even the emperor Domitian has his grapes brought to him from these very vineyards. Secondly, it is because this place has experienced two earthquakes within the last seventy years. Philadelphia had always been so prosperous up until AD17 when the first earthquake hit. The damage was so bad that Rome exempted us from paying taxes for five years! Then we had another earthquake in the AD30's and so there has always been a sense of compassion from the Roman world to us here in Philadelphia."

Had Rabah known what was going to happen next, he would not have said the good things that he did. There was a sound of many Roman chariots that stopped immediately outside Rabah's house. A Roman centurion stepped out from the chariot and came wandering across to the house. Rabah's wife pointed at Rabah, and the centurion accompanied by two soldiers came towards him.

"Leave this to me, Ekrem. I am sure this will just be about more grapes needed."

Judging by the expression on the centurion's face, Ekrem was not convinced that this band of Roman soldiers had just come to do some early morning shopping. Things looked more serious than that and Ekrem had a strange feeling on the inside that everything was about to get nasty.

"Are you Rabah?" asked the centurion. Rabah nodded. "Then order all your people to come here and out from the vineyards."

"But..." Rabah started, but then decided to just obey the Roman centurion's orders. He gave the signal to the overseers and within the next ten minutes every worker had left the vineyards.

The centurion turned to the first two soldiers that had accompanied him from the chariot. "Take Rabah to my chariot and keep him there."

"Why? What has he done?" screamed Rabah's wife. "Why are you taking my husband away?" She ran to grab at the centurion's arm, but the other soldiers crossed their spears, blocking her way.

"He hasn't done anything, miss, but I cannot allow him to stop me in my duties." The centurion turned to the entire band of soldiers waiting in the chariots. "Right! In the name of Caesar, I charge you to burn the vineyards!"

Burn the vineyards? You can't do that, thought Ekrem. *The foxes were bad enough, but not this.*

"Why?!" shouted Rabah, watching in absolute horror as the vineyards started to go up into flame, growing greater and stronger second by second, minute by minute. The workers tried to stop the soldiers, but they were too helpless. The vineyards were going to be destroyed.

It didn't take long. One minute there had been beautiful vineyards full of delicious, mouth-watering grapes. Now, it was a black field of burnt vines and smouldering fires. Smoke had filled the air.

The centurion went over to his chariot and let the distraught and sobbing Rabah come back to see the remains of the vineyards.

"Tell me why you did this?" he asked the centurion again.

"The Emperor Domitian commanded that all the vineyards in Philadelphia were to be destroyed. Yours was the last to go. The emperor will now only ever have wine grown from the imperial city of Rome. Nothing must rival it, not even Philadelphia."

Rabah spat on the ground. "Then cursed be the Emperor Domitian."

The soldiers went to cease Rabah and arrest him, but the centurion held back his hand. "Leave him! He has suffered enough for one day. Look, he is now nothing. The might of Rome will never be defeated."

Rabah fell on his knees, covering his head with the dust and soil from the ground. "Leave me! Everyone!" he shouted. "I, of all good men, have been betrayed and cursed."

*

Ekrem didn't know what to do. He was a stranger here. It was only appropriate that he should leave. *But what do I do now? Where should I go?*

"I'll tell you," came a familiar voice from behind him.

"Theophilus," said Ekrem. "Did you see what has just happened to Rabah's vineyards?"

Theophilus nodded. "It has happened to all the vineyard owners across the whole city. There is great sadness everywhere and many workers who are now without jobs."

"I hadn't thought about them," replied Ekrem. "What will they do now?"

"I don't know, Ekrem. These are bad days in Philadelphia, but we will go to the synagogue where the Jewish people meet to pray. Maybe we will find some better news there."

They walked down the narrow paths lined with palm trees, past the large stone pillars of the Roman temple to Dionysus, the god of fruitfulness and vegetation. *That's ironic,* thought Ekrem. *They worship the god of fruitfulness in this city and there he is destroying his own vineyards. It doesn't make sense.*

When they eventually arrived at the synagogue, there was an argument going on outside. Every word was being spoken in the ancient Jewish language of Hebrew, so Ekrem couldn't understand what was happening, but it seemed that one man wasn't allowing the other man to come in through the front door of the synagogue. The man blocking the door kept pointing at a necklace around the other man's neck.

"What's happening here, Theophilus?" Ekrem asked.

"He's being denied entry," replied Theophilus. "He has denounced his faith and so he is no longer allowed in."

"Can't he go somewhere else?" enquired Ekrem.

"Well, it's not that easy," replied Theophilus. "The Jewish people have an exemption from paying tribute to Caesar. Now that this man has denounced his religion, he will have to pay tribute... and by the sound of it, he doesn't want to do that either!"

The man blocking the doorway suddenly pushed the other man away and slammed the doors of the synagogue closed. This was followed by a sound of doors being locked.

Ekrem watched as the second man walked away from the doors in total disbelief. Like Rabah had done, the man fell on his face and wailed loudly. "I will not change my mind – and I will not confess Caesar as lord."

*

At that moment, Ekrem and Theophilus watched as a messenger arrived, carrying a scroll. He went up to the sobbing wreck on the ground, nudged him and gave him the scroll. The weeping man sat up, dried his face, broke the seal and unrolled the scroll. As he read, his face went from tearful to immense joy. He thanked the messenger and retained the scroll.

"Theophilus," begun Ekrem. "Can't we ask to see the scroll? It's clearly had a massive impact on the man to stop him crying and see him leaping around with joy."

Sure enough, the same man was jumping up and down and shouting with great exuberance.

"May I see?" Theophilus asked the man who agreed and handed it to him. Theophilus unrolled it and showed it to Ekrem.

"But I don't understand," said Ekrem, looking bewildered at the writing.

"You will one day," replied Theophilus, "but for the moment look at this one sentence here." He pointed at a line close to the start of the writing. It read: I have set before you an open door and no man can shut it: for you have a little strength and have kept my word and have not denied my name."

"You mean, he's not going to be shut out forever?" asked Ekrem, still confused by the message.

Theophilus looked at Ekrem with a smile. "What he loses here, he will be given bountifully by the writer of this scroll."

What an amazing friend to have, thought Ekrem, *and such incredible timing to.*

Theophilus gave the scroll back to the man and thanked him. Turning back to Ekrem, he asked, "So, what have you learnt here from your time in Philadelphia, Ekrem? What secrets did your grandfather want you to know?"

Ekrem thought long and hard. "I think there are a few secrets I can take away from here with me," he started. "Here goes:

1. Growing good fruit takes time and effort.

2. We can all face problems that are like foxes. They appear when we don't expect them, and they are a nuisance to get rid of; but if we don't deal with our problems, they will destroy all the good things in our lives.

3. Selfishness will cause people to betray one another, so be generous and not jealous.

4. Being shut out by others is horrible, so find those who are faithful and true to you."

"That's a good set of secrets," replied Theophilus. "Now what about the treasure?"

"I haven't got anything to take home with me from this place," answered Ekrem. "Had I known what was going to happen, I would have hidden some of Rabah's grapes in my pocket. Not that they would have lasted long. So, I don't know what I will be able to treasure."

Theophilus smirked. Ekrem looked around to see what his friend was smiling at. All he could see was a weary man wandering along the road in their direction; but as he got nearer, Ekrem recognised his face.

"Ekrem, my dear boy," Rabah said. "I must still pay you for the work you did for me yesterday."

"No, no," replied Ekrem. "Not after all that has happened to you today. You don't need to pay me – you really don't."

"Then I must bless you," said Rabah. "Even in times of trouble, us Jewish people offer blessings for everything. Here, Ekrem, take this..." In his hand, he held out a small bottle of wine. "This is from the grapes of our vineyard. Treasure it, Ekrem. It will be a vintage wine, believe me!"

Ekrem took the bottle of wine and the two of them hugged one another. This time, it was Ekrem who was shedding some tears. He had truly met a very humble and good man; someone he would never forget.

"Theophilus, meet Rabah..." started Ekrem, but Theophilus had completely disappeared.

*

Mehmet could suddenly hear footsteps. The room had gone dark, but he knew that Ekrem was coming closer to the door. *I had better get back to bed before he gets upstairs,* Mehmet thought to himself. He dashed up two at a time, slipped back under the covers, closed his eyes and pretended to snore heavily.

Moments later, Ekrem came into the room. He tiptoed across to Mehmet who let out an even greater pretend snore. "Are you asleep?" Ekrem asked Mehmet.

Stupid boy, thought Mehmet. *I'm not exactly going to say 'yes I am' am I? But I daren't say no either.*

Ekrem placed the bottle under his bed, climbed inside the duvet, pulled the covers over him and went off to sleep.

Candles, rugs, and now wine? thought Mehmet. *Right, I think it's time to get to the bottom of this. Once Ekrem is sound asleep, I am going to get some answers and I know exactly how to do it!*

*

Chapter 13

It only took a few minutes for Ekrem to be sound asleep. *Right,* thought Mehmet, *now's my chance to find out what is really going on!* He crept out from the bedroom, closing the door as slowly and as quietly as he could. Then tiptoeing along the corridor to Alida's room, where the door had been left ajar, he slipped in.

"Alida..." Mehmet hissed. "Alida, wake up..."

Alida woke up with a start and was even more perturbed to find Mehmet in her room. "Mehmet! What's the problem? What are you doing in here?"

"Ekrem's been in the living room but there's a problem with the candles..."

Alida threw back the covers straight away. *Obviously, there's some sort of problem,* she thought. It never occurred to her that Mehmet shouldn't know about these things. She was only half awake as it was. She quickly slipped her slippers on, and followed by Mehmet, she crept out of her room and down the stairs to the hallway. Mehmet smiled to himself – so far, his plan was working.

Alida opened the door and stepped into the darkness of the living room. "Ekrem," she whispered, "what's the problem with the candles?" There was no answer, just the sound of Mehmet closing the living room door behind them.

"The problem, Alida," started Mehmet, "is that I don't know how these candles work."

"What are you talking about, Mehmet, you trickster? where's Ekrem?"

"He's upstairs in bed fast asleep. He got back to bed about ten minutes ago. I've been watching him through the gap in the door here and I saw how he laid out the candles in a particular way and then all went dark, and he seemed to disappear. Then about ten minutes later, he was putting the candles away and then came out with a bottle of wine."

Alida couldn't believe her ears. It wasn't just the fact that her brother had come out with a bottle of wine, which she guessed had come back from wherever Ekrem had been; but that Mehmet had been watching and knew all this information.

"Let's face it, Alida," continued Mehmet. "Your brother isn't going to tell me anything. He doesn't like me. In fact, he hates my guts, so I think you had better explain how this works."

"I'm not telling you anything," replied Alida. "I'm going back to bed." She pulled at the doorknob, hoping to barge Mehmet, who was blocking the door, out of the way; but she was not strong enough against Mehmet's weight leaning against it.

"Come on, Alida, just tell me how it works. That's all I want to know."

Alida marched across the room and sat herself on the sofa, her legs up across the cushions, her arms folded and a look of defiance across her face.

"I told you I'm not going to tell you anything, so you've got a long wait, Mehmet. What happens here is none of your business."

Mehmet took a deep sigh. "Oh well..." he said casually, "I guess there's only one thing for it." He pulled a mobile phone out of his pyjama trouser pocket. The phone screen lit up as the phone started. His fingers started moving quickly across the screen like bees buzzing around the flowers.

"What are you doing now?" asked Alida suspiciously, watching Mehmet look quite pleased with himself.

"Just making a call," he replied casually. "Nothing to worry about."

"Who are you calling? If you're calling the police, then you're going to get in serious trouble for wasting their time," Alida informed Mehmet.

"Oh, I'm not calling the police," Mehmet replied, his fingers poised over the green call button. "I'm calling your home phone number."

"Why?" asked Alida, not getting up from the sofa to confront Mehmet again. "What are you hoping to achieve by doing that?"

"Simple," smiled Mehmet. "The phone will ring. Your parents will wake up and come down to answer it. I will speak to them and tell them that I found you in the living room trying to clear up wine that you've spilt on the rug here and that Ekrem is hiding another bottle in his bedroom."

"But I haven't spilt any wine on the rug," answered Alida.

"Not yet, Alida," Mehmet replied, holding a bottle of wine in his hand. "Now instead of all the trouble with your parents, why don't you just explain to me how these candles work and what they do?"

Alida realised there was no choice. Mehmet was a scheming, little rat and had planned this trick out very carefully. *I could just shout and wake everybody up,* she contemplated, *but then Mehmet will probably just pour the wine over the rug and the same consequence will still come about. I shall have to tell him how the candles work. Hopefully nothing will happen.* She paused. *Ekrem will be so annoyed when he finds out.*

*

Alida set out the saucers and the candles on the rug whilst Mehmet continued barricading the door. She lit the candles and went and stood next to one of the ones marked with an 'S'. She picked it up, the room went dark, and both the living room and Mehmet disappeared.

Mehmet couldn't believe his eyes. Alida had actually disappeared from the room. He checked all around the furniture in case this was some nasty trick she had played in retaliation; but no, Alida had gone, and it wasn't through the door. *Right,* he thought to himself, *I don't know what happens next, but I'm going to do the same.* He relit all the candles and then copying the exact same method as Alida had done, he picked up the same candle with the letter 'S'. Everything went dark and the living room disappeared.

Alida found herself stood in front of some Corinthian style columns of a building that resembled some kind of temple or something. There were archways along the back and two different levels. Most of the columns were still intact. The only thing that was mainly missing was the front of the building. She looked to the left and the right-hand side of the building but there were just ruins. This was the only structure still standing. *Where am I?* Alida pondered. *I have never seen a place like this before. I shall have to find out more about it when I get home.*

"Remember me?" came a voice from behind her.

Alida swung around. "Kayra!" she shouted. "How good to see you again. What are you doing here?"

"I've come to help you, of course," Kayra replied. "But you might need these as well." She held out a pair of glasses that resembled some very funky sunglasses. "These are high powered technological glasses that enable you to see the activity that would have gone on in any given historical site that you might go to."

"Wow!" exclaimed Alida. "That's amazing." She slipped on the glasses and immediately there were Roman people wandering about, doing all manner of activities and work.

"Let's start over to the side of this building," suggested Kayra. "We'll come back here in a minute." For the next hour or so, Kayra gave Alida an explanation of all that was happening in the Roman time. Alida was astonished that Kayra knew so much, and yet at the same time, everything Kayra said was happening (thanks to the glasses) right in front of her eyes.

*

The place was called Sardis, known nowadays as Sart, and was that of an ancient city that was liberated by Alexander the Great in 340BC when he developed it into a Greek city. By the time the Romans took possession of the area, the worship of the goddess Artemis was the main focus of the city. Not only that though, but the city also had a large synagogue for Jewish people to worship in too. The area was known for its wealth and therefore the Romans valued it highly. Although there were many different people groups here, Christians, Jews, pagans, Romans and more, everyone in Sardis wanted to forget about their differences and just get along. For people to have differences of opinion was not acceptable, so there were lots of 'agreeing to disagree' conversations or dropping of one's own beliefs and ideas to accept others.

"Everyone is right, and no-one is wrong," Alida witnessed one man saying to another. "It's the best way to live without arguments and disagreements. Even my wife agrees!" The man and his companion laughed.

"Do you agree with them, Alida?" Kayra asked her with a serious expression on her face.

"Well... I like the idea that everybody gets along. That does make life easier; but I am not sure that he should be saying that everyone is right, and no-one is wrong because we all make mistakes sometimes. It would be like me saying that $4 \times 3 = 14$ when we all know it's not."

"Good answer", replied Kayra.

They started walking around the site until they eventually came back to the building that Alida had found herself stood in front of when she arrived – the one with the two levels and all the columns. She let out a little squeal when she saw what it was, and quickly removed the glasses.

"Kayra, it's a gymnasium right next door to a synagogue." Kayra nodded. "And...and...and..." Alida could hardly get the words out. "And...they're all naked!"

"Yes, Alida," replied Kayra. "That's what they did here in the Roman days."

"But what about the upstairs level? Were they just spectating galleries?"

Kayra nodded. "Yes, they were, and behind there used to be bedrooms for people to stay in."

"Weren't the Jewish people a little upset with the gymnasium next door to their synagogue? I mean, it must have disturbed them," suggested Alida.

"Not quite," replied Kayra. "You must remember that everyone here in Sardis lived with a 'get-along-with-each-other' mentality, so even the Jewish people would go to the gymnasium straight after synagogue."

*

Kayra led Alida across the road to another set of stones and pillars that clearly were part of another large building at one time.

"Put your glasses back on, Alida," instructed Kayra, "and then you will see more about this place too."

Alida put them on and immediately saw that they were standing inside the temple of Artemis. Here Alida saw people making sacrifices to this goddess with animals, plants, gemstones, metals and other gifts in silver, white, green and red. Prayers were being offered up and songs sung in praise of what a wonderful goddess she was.

Further along the road was the agora, the marketplace with stone structures with etchings of crosses, menorahs and laurels. *A real mix of cultures,* thought Alida, *all believing their own things but all accepting each other's ideas and practices too.*

"Would you have wanted to live here in the Roman times, Kayra?" asked Alida, wanting to learn Kayra's opinions of all that was going on around her; but Kayra had disappeared.

Alida looked down. The glasses were still in her hand. *At least I have something to take back with me to show Ekrem.* Another dreadful thought that hit her mind. *What about Mehmet? Where was he?* She thought about all the things she had seen and heard during her time in Sardis. *Everyone seemed to get along with everyone here. Mehmet couldn't cause many problems, could he?*

Little did Alida know what Mehmet was going to get caught up in.

*

Mehmet didn't know what was happening to him. One minute he was stood in the living room with Alida, and the next he was standing inside a historical city protected by some very heavy fortifications. On the walls were some soldiers with spears, shields, boots and helmets. *From my limited knowledge of history,* thought Mehmet, *these soldiers look like they belong* to an army that existed way before the Greek and Roman empires.

Looking around, the soldiers on the fortified walls looked most fierce and also on high alert. They were poised ready for action at any given moment. *I wonder if I can join them,* contemplated Mehmet. *I like a good battle.*

"Boy! You, there! What are you doing?" shouted one of the soldiers from the ramparts. "Get over here immediately."

I'd better obey, thought Mehmet. *He looks a bit scary to argue with. Worse than the P.E. teacher at school. I wouldn't want him teaching me rugby or something.*

He planned to walk casually but then thought that marching across might be more appropriate. On arrival at the soldier, he saluted as he had seen the British soldiers do on the television at the Cenotaph on Remembrance Sunday.

"What are you doing, boy?!" yelled the soldier.

"I'm saluting," replied Mehmet, hoping to impress the soldier with his knowledge of military conduct.

"Salivating more like," replied the soldier. "Can't you see the predicament we're in? Look out there."

Mehmet stood on his toes to look over the top of the walls. Sure enough, down at the base of the hill was a fierce looking army. They were preparing for battle and every one of them was intent on breaking through the walls. Mehmet looked back at the soldier. "Hmm..." he nodded. "You certainly have a problem."

"What do you mean 'you have a problem'?" bellowed the soldier. "Don't you mean 'we have a problem'? Whose side are you on?"

Mehmet's brain thought fast. "Yours of course," he replied rapidly, not wanting to anger the soldier or find himself run through with a spear as an imposter for the enemy – after all, he had only just appeared from nowhere.

"Right then, now you get down off these walls and get back to your family. This is no place for a young man like you. You might get hurt or killed."

"Good idea," replied Mehmet. The thought of being injured or dying when he was so far away from home was not a good one. *Besides they might not even have doctors or hospitals here to make me better.* He nodded to the soldier and went off to find the nearest steps to the ground level.

*

The rest of the day was quite boring. Everyone in the city was on tenterhooks for fear of the invading army outside the walls. The only excitement came when a horn sounded to say that a royal decree was about to be made. Mehmet watched as people gathered together to listen to the message. The messenger declared how King Croesus *(whoever he is,* thought Mehmet) had insisted that no-one should leave the city for any reason whatsoever. Anyone who tried to leave would bring about certain defeat for both the army and the city. The people replied with some response that Mehmet didn't understand, but it sounded agreeable.

The people went back to their everyday lives more nervous than ever, and Mehmet went wandering to find something to eat.

"I will be glad when Cyrus' army is gone from outside our walls," said one man to a trader selling fruit and olives.

"Yes, so will I," replied the trader. "The gods help anyone who betrays this city of Sardis to Cyrus. We'll all be dead."

They both looked at Mehmet who happened to be standing there feeling quite hopeless and helpless. "And it better not be you!" they said.

*

Chapter 14

Mehmet was not enjoying his visit to this fortress at all. He sat contemplating what he had learnt about his situation so far: there was a king called Croesus who ruled this city. The city was called Sardis. There was an enemy army outside led by someone called Cyrus. Apparently, the year was 547BC; and the only friend he had made was a vicious looking soldier up on the walls.

I can't see what's so great about coming to places like this. Stupid old candles. Stupid old rug. What's the point of it all? Why did I even bother to go to all that trouble of pestering Alida? Aside from that, I don't know what Ekrem's going to say when I get back. If I get back... How do I get out of here?

"Hi Ekrem," came a voice from behind him. "You're looking different somehow."

Mehmet turned around to look at the person speaking. It was another boy of about his own age. "You know Ekrem?" he asked.

"Yes, I know Ekrem," replied Theophilus, "and you're not him. Who are you?"

"My name's Mehmet," he answered, putting out his fist to do a fist bump.

Theophilus looked at him very strangely. "Ekrem didn't tell me he had a twin brother."

"Twin brother? No, he doesn't. I'm a friend of his..." Mehmet looked down shamefully. "Well, actually, no

I'm not a friend of his; I'm just in his class at school...and well... I tricked Ekrem's sister into getting me here...and um, well, here I am..."

Theophilus looked most annoyed. "You're a traitor, Mehmet – and I don't deal with traitors. You will certainly be getting no help from me. Just give this item to Ekrem when you return. He will have to find out for himself what it means." He handed Mehmet a scroll.

"Who shall I say it's from?" asked Mehmet, but the boy in front of him just vanished into thin air right in front of his eyes. "Where did he go? Where did he go?"

*

Mehmet was tempted to open the scroll and read it. It wasn't a very big scroll – about the length of a teaspoon. *It can't say very much,* he thought. Still his conscience was starting to kick in and he decided to keep the scroll sealed. It might help as a peace offering between him and Ekrem.

The day seemed to be dragging and Mehmet decided that he would go back to see the soldier on the wall who had spoken to him earlier. *At least I'll have some company,* he thought to himself, *and I can watch what Cyrus' army are getting up to.*

The soldier didn't seem too pleased to see Mehmet back again. "Nothing happened so far, boy," said the soldier. "Hopefully, everything stays that way. Haven't you got a home to go to?"

Mehmet shook his head. "No, I don't," he replied. "I'm a stranger here."

"Well, looking at those clothes you're wearing I would say you're a stranger here. Not only that but you're a strange stranger." He gave out a little laugh.

Clearly this soldier has a sense of humour. Perhaps we could share some jokes whilst we're waiting for something to happen. He racked his brain quickly.

"Where does Cyrus keep his armies?" Mehmet asked.

"Down there," replied the soldier, "although I wish he'd hurry up and move them."

Mehmet looked at the soldier with a most disapproving stare. "No, no, no, you don't understand, I'm telling you a joke. You know, like a funny story. I say the first line and then you say, 'I don't know' and then I tell you the funny bit, and you laugh."

The soldier looked utterly confused. "Do we need to do this?" he asked. "I'm doing an important job here defending this city."

"But they're not doing anything down there, are they?" responded Mehmet, observing that Cyrus' army were no longer on standby and were busy cooking food over open fires and sharpening their weapons. "Now then, where does Cyrus keep his armies?"

"I don't know," recalled the soldier, repeating the words in the same way that Mehmet had told him.

"Up his sleevies," laughed Mehmet, pulling on his sleeves. "Get it? Arm-ies? Sleeve-ies?"

The soldier laughed and then promptly said, "No."

I've got to get this soldier to understand a joke, determined Mehmet. *Life is too boring otherwise.* "Okay," he said, "let's try another one. Two soldiers are standing on a wall. The first one says, 'Look a dead bird' and the second one looks up in the sky and says 'Where?'." Mehmet started laughing.

The soldier looked up in the sky and then realised that dead birds don't fly. He started laughing and laughing. He laughed so much that his helmet came off and dropped over the wall.

"Now look what you've done!" he roared at Mehmet. "I can't stay here without my helmet; and it's fallen outside the city walls so I can't get it. No-one is allowed out of the city."

"Don't worry," replied Mehmet reassuringly. "I think I can help. Come with me." He beckoned his hand and the soldier turned to follow him.

*

Earlier that day, Mehmet had found a doorway hidden behind some rather tangled up greenery in the lower ramparts of the wall. He hadn't intended to find it but had been absolutely desperate to relieve himself; and so, had considered that the only place was somewhere hidden and unseen. On having relieved himself, he had then noticed the old wooden door that looked as if it had been sealed closed since the fortress surrounding the city had first been built. He had tried tugging at the door to open it, but the door was locked by a large wooden beam going across it into a rather large slab of stone wall on the other end. Mehmet hadn't been strong enough to open it, but surely the soldier would be strong enough.

The soldier mumbled as he pushed his way through the greenery. "You'd better not be taking me on some foolish mission, or I will slice you up like roasted lamb meat," he threatened; but as Mehmet guided him through, he noticed the door with a look of absolute amazement.

"I didn't even know this door was here," he said.

"Well, your helmet can't be far away on the other side from here," said Mehmet.

The soldier took hold of the wooden beam and, with great force and might, slid the beam across and started to pull the creaky door a little ajar. "Stay here," he said.

What happened next was disastrous. The soldier retrieved his helmet with no problems, but Cyrus' army spotted what was happening. Within hours, the invading army had changed location to the opposite side of the city. From here they launched an attack on Sardis, distracting Croesus' soldiers and making them focus on the side of the fortress opposite to the secret door. Then, all of a sudden, a small covert group of invaders came through the secret door and into the fortress.

There were screams and cries as the people of Sardis were taken by surprise. Nothing could stop the invasion of Cyrus' armies now who had waited for ages for this opportunity.

"Get me out of here, get me out of here," cried Mehmet, who was convinced that either Cyrus' army would get him or the soldier whose helmet he had knocked off. Then in a split second, everything for Mehmet changed. The soldiers disappeared, the invading army disappeared, and Mehmet found himself stood alone in the same location.

What is going on here? Everyone's disappeared, but I am still stood here alone in the city.

A deep, booming voice started to speak. "Mehmet..."

Mehmet looked around but couldn't see anyone. The voice called his name again, but it seemingly came from nowhere. It sounded authoritative, powerful and directive. "Mehmet, do you see what happened to the city of Sardis?" Mehmet nodded. "Now watch and see what happens to this city, not just once, but twice."

The roaring voice faded, and, in a flash, people started to appear all around him. The first observation that Mehmet made however was that the people weren't the same as the ones previously. The soldiers' attire was different. The city had in itself seemed to have changed and advanced a little.

"Excuse me," Mehmet said to a passer-by, carrying a bundle of hay on his back. "Is Croesus still king of Sardis?"

The man laughed. "Don't you know your history, boy? King Croesus was here about two hundred and fifty years ago. That's when Cyrus' army came and attacked the city."

"Yes, I know," nodded Mehmet sadly. There was a pause. "So, what's the situation now?"

"Well…" the man started, "we are much more secure nowadays than back then. The fortress and city of Sardis is better fortified and, as you will see, although there is the Persian army outside of our walls, they can't break through."

Not again, thought Mehmet. *Not another enemy invasion of Sardis.* Then he remembered the words that the roaring voice had said to him. "See what happens to this city – not just once, but twice." *Oh no! I know what's going to happen here.*

"Listen carefully everyone," cried Mehmet aloud to anyone who might listen. "The Persian army are going to take this city unless you are very careful. Just as happened with King Croesus, the same is going to happen again."

"What's the boy talking about?" said one woman with a most annoyed and indignant look on her face. She put down the vegetables that she was carrying. "You be careful what scary nonsense you are putting in peoples' minds," she warned Mehmet.

"No, it's true – it will happen," cried Mehmet.

"What are you, a prophet?" sneered another.

"No… I'm just a boy who can foresee the future. If I had the chance, I would get my history book from home and show you what happens."

"Go on then," shouted another. "Run home and prove it to us."

"But I can't," yelled back Mehmet. "I don't know how to get home."

"And you don't know what you're talking about either!" said another. "Shut your nonsense and stop worrying. We'll be fine. Peace, Peace, nothing but peace. The Persians will soon realise they're not coming in here."

Mehmet drooped his head with dismay. He knew they were wrong. *How foolish to be promising peace when disaster is inevitable!*

*

The Persians outside of the city had been observing Sardis for a long time. The city was indeed well fortified, but they knew that there had to come a moment to strike. Flying above the city were hungry vultures searching for dead animals that had been thrown over the wall to decompose or become vulture food. The vultures would swoop down, take their fill of dead animal and then ascend high back into the air until the next 'feeding time'.

"Look," cried one of the Persians. "Look at those vultures over there at that spot on the side of the fortress just by the city wall. The vultures have flown in, but they aren't leaving again. They just circle and fly immediately back down. There's something strange about that spot and we need to find out what."

That night, the Persians set out to go investigate that particular part of the wall. Under the cover of darkness, they discovered a weakness. This was the part of the city where the dead bodies were thrown over from those who had died in Sardis. The wall was weaker and less protected. *Right,* the Persians agreed, *this is the point to attack.*

*

Mehmet watched with disbelief as the Persians came against the city and broke through the walls of Sardis. It felt like he was watching a replay of an action film and it brought him great sadness to see the fear, the aggression, the tension and the pain all over again. Normally, had it been a film, it wouldn't have moved him; but watching events like this in real life really did tug at the heart strings. This time he didn't cry out to leave as quickly as possible. He felt as if he were merely a spectator to the tragedy of life, but not a victim. *You can choose to be a victim,* he had once heard someone say, *or you can choose to be a spectator, watching what's going on, experiencing the oppression and the pain, but never giving into defeat.*

Moments later, Sardis disappeared, and he found himself back in the living room of Ekrem's household. It was dark and he was about to pick up the candles to replace them when, to his shock, the living room lights came on and there in front of him was Ekrem, Alida and their parents; and this time, Alida was blocking the door!

*

Chapter 15

Ekrem and Alida's father broke the silence. He hadn't been pleased at all to be woken up by his children shortly after midnight. "So then, what's happening here then, Mehmet?"

Mehmet looked highly embarrassed. What could he say? What explanation could he give to Ekrem and Alida's parents? *They're not going to believe me whatever I say,* he thought to himself, *and if I tell them about the rug and the candles and everything, they're just going to think I'm crazy; and if I tell them about Ekrem and the wine, they won't believe me either.*

"Ekrem tells me that you were helping yourself to some wine," continued Father. "It appears you have found yourself a bottle," pointing at the one on the floor which Mehmet had held earlier. "Alida tells me that she found you creeping around here; that she was going to come and tell us; but you blocked the door from coming out, until you decided to look for the wine and that's when she came and awoke us and your brother."

"I am most disappointed, Mehmet," said Ekrem and Alida's mother. "It's not the kind of behaviour your parents are going to want to hear about, but I will have to tell them. None of us want you becoming addicted to drink at this age, do we?"

Everyone shook their heads.

"Now I suggest," Father continued, "that you, Mehmet, return the wine to where you found it and get straight back to bed. The same for you two as well," he said, pointing at Ekrem and Alida. "I don't want another sound from anyone for the rest of the night. Now, do you have any last thing to say, Mehmet?"

"I'm sorry," said Mehmet. *I don't mean it,* he thought, *but what can I do in a situation like this?*

*

"Snitch!" Mehmet hissed at Alida as they went upstairs.

"Idiot!" said Ekrem, looking fiercely at Mehmet. "I knew you were trouble. Serves you right! You won't be staying here again - I can promise you that."

"You haven't had the last laugh yet," replied Mehmet bluffing as hard as possible to still make himself look tough, yet on the inside he was feeling the most intimidated he had ever felt in his life.

"And what's that supposed to mean?" Ekrem replied with a look of burning fire blazing in his eyes. *Any more nonsense from you, Mehmet, and I will make sure everyone at school knows about you and the wine thieving,* but he didn't say it aloud.

Alida changed the subject. "So, what was it like anyway? Did you go to Sardis?"

"Yes, I did, and it was horrendous! Loads of armies, fighting, killing and more."

"That's unusual," replied Ekrem. "There's not normally war or anything in the places I've been to."

"Well, count yourselves fortunate then," mumbled Mehmet. "Oh, by the way, I was told to give you this."

He pulled the little scroll out of his pocket and handed it to Ekrem who immediately broke the seal and unrolled it. He read the few words on the parchment carefully and then smiled.

"What does it say?" asked Alida, fascinated and curious at what had made Ekrem smile so much.

Ekrem showed her the scroll, and her face went from being serious to that of a smirk.

"What? What? What does it say?!" demanded Mehmet.

Ekrem turned the scroll around and showed him the eight words written on it. They read: ***I will come upon you like a thief.***

Mehmet stared at it. "That's what happened in Sardis," he started. "Cyrus and his armies came against the city like a thief when they discovered a secret entrance to a door in the wall; and then it happened again two hundred or so years later when the Persians also came against Sardis. Both times the city was lost because the invading armies crept in unexpectedly."

"Well, if you ask me," said Ekrem still smirking alongside Alida, "it sounds like you, Mehmet!"

*

The next morning was Saturday. Mehmet left about 9:30am. His parents were not pleased to hear that Mehmet had been trying to steal wine from his kind hosts across the road. As much as Mehmet tried to convince his parents that he hadn't been stealing wine, they didn't believe him.

"You won't be staying away again for a while," Mehmet's father told him. "I can't afford you getting our family a bad reputation in this neighbourhood. You will be grounded for the next month."

I will get revenge, thought Mehmet. *I don't know how I will do it yet, but you'll be sorry. Somehow, I shall get rid of that time travelling rug of yours!*

*

"So... what did you learn from your time in Sardis?" Ekrem later asked Alida when he knew that their parents were out of earshot.

"Well," Alida started. "It was mainly Kayra's glasses that helped tremendously to see how things would have been in the past. Today, of course, it's just another ruins, but there's more standing than in some of the other locations. But in answer to your question, I think the secrets are:

1. That diverse cultures can all exist peacefully together.

2. That you shouldn't compromise on your own beliefs.

3. That people can think they are right even if they are completely wrong; we shouldn't judge them for being wrong but help them to come to the truth.

4. And from what Mehmet said, the enemy can come like a thief in the night to steal, kill and destroy. We must be careful therefore that our weak spots don't become entrances of destruction."

"Great thoughts, Alida – and I didn't even come, but I feel like I have learnt so much from your visit to

Sardis," answered Ekrem. "Do you think we will be able to persuade our parents to let us visit the town of Sart one day so I can see the ruins for myself?"

Alida nodded. "I expect so, after all, there's no reason for them to suspect anything. We can both convince them that we have an interest in the history of our land. Not only that, but our history teacher will be really pleased."

*

Ekrem's father and mother woke both Ekrem and Alida early the following morning. "Come on, you two, we need to up and going this morning."

"Why?" asked Ekrem, turning over in his bed, still clutching the pillow tightly. "I am so tired. Why do we need to get up so early?"

"Haven't you remembered what day it is?"

Ekrem thought hard. He hadn't really been paying attention to the calendar as such. His mind had been far too busy concentrating on the secrets and treasures left by Grandpa. He still couldn't think of the answer with his tired mind.

"It's the 1st of Muharram," his father said. "That means we shall have a special family day out to celebrate the new Islamic year."

"Can we go to the village of Sart?" Ekrem asked, remembering his conversation from the night before.

"No," answered his mother, "we don't want to go to some small village; we want to see some sights in the city. We're going to visit Izmir. Now, come on, you and Alida."

It wasn't long before they were all ready and climbing into the car ready to go on a day's outing. The journey would not take long. It was only 82-83 km or so and therefore would take about an hour and 40 minutes if the traffic was all clear.

Ekrem and Alida hadn't been to Izmir since they were both small and so both of them forgot about anything else and just looked forward to an exciting day. Their minds thought about shopping, food, drink, city life... until another thought came into their minds. "Is there any historical remains in Izmir?" asked Alida. "I'm getting quite interested in Turkish history now."

"Yes, so am I," added Ekrem, wanting to back Alida up as quickly as possible.

"Well, there may be some places to visit; but we do already have an exciting day lined up for you both."

Ekrem and Alida both felt disappointed on the inside that they wouldn't be visiting any historical sites; but they were determined not to show it or appear ungrateful for what promised to be a really good day. Just having time together as a whole family to enjoy a day out was so precious, particularly when both their parents worked so awfully hard during the week.

*

The day itself did fly by. It started by going to the Kemeralti market which had so many interesting things to look at and buy.

"Don't spend all your money here," advised their father. "There's plenty more to see."

The market itself dated back to the 17th century linking and ancient agora to Konak Square. Throughout the whole market were shops and eating places, tea gardens, mosques, synagogues, hidden courtyards and artisan workshops. There was so much to see!

Armed full of carrier bags, they returned to the car at about 3pm. "Don't put anything in the boot of the car. I didn't have time to empty it. You'll have to take all your shopping in the back seat with you. Right, let's go," said their father. "Next stop, the Arkas Art Centre."

The Arkas Art Centre. Well, Ekrem and Alida couldn't believe it. They had heard about this place from their art teacher at school who was always raving on about how brilliant it was, but they never expected to actually be visiting it.

The art centre itself was incredible, boutique and beautiful. There were famous paintings, sculptures and musical instruments that were of such superb quality.

"This is amazing!" exclaimed Alida, "I feel so inspired to be artistic and produce things like this."

"You should do," her mother replied. "You should always take hold of opportunities when they arise. When something touches your heart, Alida, you should never hold back."

*

It took a long time to go around the arts centre admiring all the wonderful work as well as the lovely décor and architecture of the centre itself. But eventually, Ekrem, Alida and their parents wandered wearily back to the car.

"I'm so tired!" Ekrem said, yawning rather too loudly.

"Well, we still have one more surprise for you," said their father. "You'll find out about it in about 15 minutes."

"I'm too tired to see anymore," sighed Alida, her eyeballs nearly closing. "I'll just have a little doze. Wake me up when we get to wherever we are going."

When she was awoken about fifteen minutes later, the car had pulled up in a main street in the city. Mother and Father had got out and Ekrem had reluctantly followed them. Alida looked at the buildings around them. "I don't see anything special," she said.

"The hotel," replied their parents. "We are staying the night!"

"But we haven't got our things," protested Alida.

Their father rushed to the boot of the car and opened it. There inside were suitcases already packed. "Daa-daa," he announced. "I told you the boot of the car was full!"

*

"Brrrrring!" the doorbell on the front door of Ekrem's house went, but there was no answer. The two men stood there for a few minutes, hoping that someone would appear.

"Try again, Berkay" said the older man, "I was assured that someone would be there."

Berkay rang the bell again, but once again, there was no answer. "I told you there's no-one there!" he said. "Now what do you want to do?"

"Leave my card," replied the older man. "Hopefully, they will give us a ring."

"What if they don't?" Berkay questioned. "What will you do then, Mr. Devrim?"

"I will be sending you back here to ring the bell again," replied Mr. Devrim, looking contemptuously at his young, skinny employee. "Now put my card through the door. They'll call us, you'll see!"

*

Chapter 16

The next morning, Ekrem, Alida and their parents were sat having breakfast in the hotel restaurant when the subject of the events of the day ahead was being discussed.

"Right today, I was planning to go to the Izmir Wildlife Park," announced their father, looking intently at both Ekrem and Alida on the opposite side of the table. "I was thinking you two young people would enjoy that."

Ekrem and Alida looked at each other. It was courteous and right within the culture to follow their father's leading and guidance; but at the same time, they really wanted to find out some history of the place. *We will need to do this tactfully,* thought Ekrem. *Somehow, we need Father to change his mind for himself.*

"Do you know how long the wildlife park has been here?" Ekrem asked his father. "Do you think it would date back 50 years, 100 years, 200 years or how much?"

"That's a rather unusual question, Ekrem," replied his father. "I don't know but I am sure we will find out the answer when we get there." There was a pause. "Why have you suddenly become so interested in history? And you, Alida."

Ekrem and Alida looked at each other with a knowing look. *Perhaps now is the time to say something about their discoveries,* they both were thinking.

"Well, it was Grandpa that put us onto it," began Ekrem quite enthusiastically. "Since he died, his interest in treasures and secrets from the past has become more fascinating, and so Alida and I have been busy finding out all sorts of things."

"Give me an example," said their father. "I would be interested to hear what you have found out so far."

So, for the next half an hour or more, Ekrem and Alida started to share the history of sites like Ephesus, Sart (near the site of Sardis), Goncali (near the site of Laodicea), Alasehir (the site of Philadelphia) and Thyatira in the city of Akhisar. They were both very careful to not mention about the rug and the candles, or the fact that they had seen first-hand for themselves what had been happening back in time; but they shared with so much enthusiasm and knowledge that their parents were both overwhelmingly impressed.

"You must have spent ages researching," said their mother. "It's amazing what technology can teach you now-a-days."

Ekrem and Alida chuckled. *If only they really knew.*

"Well," said their father when Ekrem and Alida had run out of information and needed to take a breather, "I don't see much point going to the animal park after all. You are both far more interested in history. I shall find out from the hotel reception where we can go to learn some more."

Yes! Perfect! Ekrem and Alida thought to themselves.

*

It was about an hour later when they arrived at the Agora Open Air Museum. The site was enormous, magnificent and very exciting. There were large stone pillars standing tall and erect showing the size of the agora. Ekrem and Alida could just imagine the people from the Roman and Greek times trading in this place, selling many of the goods that they had seen in the other agora. Down below the 21st Century floor level however were ancient walkways that were exposed to the elements but overshadowed by the most magnificent stone arches. Narrow channels of water went through the middle of these walkways, transporting the water from one place to another. Alida and her mother stood watching the water for ages, admiring its cleanliness as well as enjoying the sound of the trickling streams. Above, where Ekrem and his father were looking down in between the arches, were gorgeous flowers in arrays of assorted colours that were so pleasing to the eye. This had simply been the best historical site that Ekrem or Alida had been to yet.

As they looked at some of the information regarding this agora, they discovered that this city was once known as Smyrna.

On hearing this fact, Alida quickly pulled Ekrem aside and whispered to him, "Ekrem, what if this site is the other place beginning with 'S' on the rug? Wouldn't that be exciting? You would get to see this very location in the past!" Ekrem subsequently became extremely excited. He couldn't wait to explore everything and everywhere about this location detail for detail. He pulled out a notebook from his pocket and carefully started making sketches of layouts, stones, water channels and much more.

Another visitor to the site couldn't help but notice Ekrem being so meticulous about the stones, the pillars and the site overall.

"Excuse me, young man, you seem very interested in all that you are seeing here," he commented.

"He is," replied Ekrem's father, "and his sister too."

"Well, perhaps I could tell you some more information then. I am a local tour guide here in Izmir, but at present, my group has gone for lunch, so I am just spending some time out here in the open air. What would you like to know?"

"Everything!" said Ekrem, followed by Alida, who had now come to join them.

*

For the next hour, the tour guide told them about how Smyrna had a strong history. It had originally been built as a city, but by 600BC or so, it had diminished to the size of a small village. When Alexander the Great arrived, he had it rebuilt into a great city.

"You see," said the tour guide, "in a sense this city that had become dead was once more alive again, and that brought the people here in Smyrna a lot of joy and hope for their future."

He continued to tell them that Smyrna got its name due to the import and export of myrrh, a plant used for burial duties. "This," he explained, "was very important later on during the Roman times when there was much persecution, torture and tribulation in this place. Many good people died here, including the famous Polycarp."

Ekrem and Alida looked at each other with confusion. "Polycarp?! I've never heard of Polycarp. It sounds like a cross between a parrot and a fish."

The tour guide took a deep breath. "In the second century AD there was a man called Polycarp. He was imprisoned for a long time for going against the Roman emperors and gods. He was well respected by many people here in Smyrna and so the Romans eventually decided to have him killed. They tried to burn him to death, but the flames would not touch him. It's a remarkable story."

"It sounds like it," said Ekrem. "Did Polycarp eventually die from old age?"

"No," replied the tour guide. "The Romans did kill him in the end, but his death was a tragic loss to the people living in Smyrna."

"I don't think I would have wanted to be around at that time," responded Ekrem.

"Sometimes, young man, terrible things happen to good people. It's not because they have done something wrong; and in Polycarp's case, it was because he stood up for what he believed even if it cost him his life."

"Thank you," replied Ekrem. "I shall remember that."

*

When the family eventually got home, their mother went and prepared the evening meal; their father went and unloaded the cases from the car and then went to spend some time sorting through the mail that had arrived over the last few days; Ekrem went to do some more research on his computer about the ancient ruins of Smyrna; and Alida went and sorted through all the wonderful items she had bought from the Kemeralti Market.

The meal that evening was delicious. Mother had cooked Ekrem's favourite dinner – Imam bayildi with barbeque lamb and tzatziki – a delicious meal of barbequed lamb mixed with vegetables and presented in a bed of aubergines with Greek yoghurt, cucumber and mint poured over the top. This was followed by Alida's favourite dessert – Turkish yoghurt cake made with nutritious figs, orange blossom water and the zest of a lemon or two.

Their stomachs were quite full by the time they went up to bed after what had been a busy couple of days.

"I'm not sure I can get up tonight and go travelling," said Alida. "Besides, it's no good me going on the 'S' symbol because if it is Smyrna, then I am only going to end up in the same place as we visited earlier today.

You can go there back in time if you want, Ekrem, then you can tell me all about it."

"I agree. I feel so tired," replied Ekrem. "I shall just see how awake I feel at midnight – that's if I'm not asleep of course," he added, stating the obvious.

*

As much as Ekrem had tried to get to sleep, his brain was just full of the notes, diagrams and memories from the time at the Agora Open Air Museum, the remains of Smyrna. When therefore the clock read 11:55pm, he couldn't stay in bed any longer. He dragged himself downstairs as quietly as possible, closed the living room door and set out the candles as usual. Having lit them all, he picked up the other candle beginning with 'S'. *Oh well,* he thought to himself, *here goes!* The room went dark, and the living room disappeared.

When Ekrem arrived, he was delighted to find that he was in the same location as they had been earlier. *So... it was Smyrna,* he told himself. *Alida will be so pleased when I tell her.* Sure enough, as he took in the sights, the columns were all in the right places; the walkways with the water channels were as he had drawn; and the agora was as he had calculated. *Wow! This is amazing! Fancy having had the opportunity to see it in real life before travelling back in time.* He decided to wander through the streets again but seeing them with a vastly different perspective. This time there were people, soldiers, traders, chariots, horses and much more. Ekrem noticed how noisy the place now seemed. *Of course,* he thought to himself, *when you're visiting ruins, you never realise how noisy and busy the places would have been in real life.*

"So… you are back again, I see," said a voice from behind him. For a moment Ekrem thought it might have been the tour guide again, ready to escort him around the city. *How foolish,* contemplated Ekrem. *The tour guide wouldn't be back here, would he?* As he turned, there was a familiar face, but one that looked quite worried. It was Theophilus.

"Theophilus, good to see you," Ekrem started, but there was no warmth radiating from Theophilus. "What's the problem? You look really downcast."

"I'm sorry, Ekrem," apologised Theophilus. "I don't mean to be unsociable; it's just that you have arrived at a challenging time. The Romans have become quite hostile more recently here in Smyrna and I am trying to help a family of refugees that are staying here for a short while here in Smyrna, but they still face potential danger. I must help them."

"Then I will help too," responded Ekrem. "I am sure there is something that can be done."

*

Theophilus led the way to a small house on the outskirts of the city. On arrival, he knocked on the door with a secret knock. The door was immediately opened, and they both walked in. The door was promptly closed again and locked behind them. Ekrem couldn't help but notice that there was a fish sign drawn into the dust outside the door.

"The fish is called an Icthus fish," explained Theophilus. "It is a secret symbol for some of us, but the Romans don't know that. They suspect it symbolises a fisherman's household, we hope.

Ekrem looked around the room. He saw a family of five, two adults and three children, all looking quite apprehensive. "Don't worry," said Theophilus, noticing that all five were staring at Ekrem. "He isn't associated to the Romans. You don't need to fear him. Let me introduce Ekrem."

The family welcomed Ekrem into their home and they sat down for a simple meal of grilled fish and bread accompanied by cups of water.

"So, what's the situation?" Ekrem asked, eager to know how he could help. "Where are you refugees from?"

"We are refugees from Damascus", the father of the family replied. "We are fleeing from the Jews and the Romans who had sent a battalion of soldiers to kill our people. So far, we have made it here to Smyrna, but it is our hope to travel from here across the water to Macedonia and settle in Thessaloniki or somewhere like that. The Romans still occupy the land there, but there will be little hatred from the Jews so we may be alright."

"Is there I can do to help you?" Ekrem asked the family. "The sun is beginning to go down. I can go out and buy supplies if you want. I can return here in the early dusk and without suspicion."

The family explained that they were short of bread and grapes. Theophilus told Ekrem whereabouts in the agora he could find a trader who would sell him what they needed. He passed a couple of coins to Ekrem who looked at them intently. The two coins were quite different from one another. The first had the symbol of a crown on it.

"What's this crown about?" he asked.

"It's the symbol of the city here in Smyrna," Theophilus answered, "but it's also a sign of victory for the games that are competed and the festival winners. Not only that, but the Emperor Domitian wears a crown himself of course."

Ekrem nodded to show he understood. The second coin was different and had a picture of a child sat on a globe and above him were seven stars. "What's this all about?" he asked.

"That coin," replied Theophilus, "was commissioned by the Emperor Domitian in AD83 when his infant son died. The emperor had his son deified and so the picture shows his son being a god over all the world and the seven stars symbolise his supreme power, but it's such a lie. We don't believe that Domitian's son has the power to rule the world, nor Domitian for that matter. The only group exempt from paying tribute to the Romans are the Jewish people and we aren't Jewish either."

Ekrem looked at the family again. They seemed so genuine, so hospitable. *Surely the Jews and the Romans couldn't hate this family, could they?*

*

Chapter 17

Ekrem's mind couldn't help but think about the refugees and immigrants he had seen on the television. He remembered how his geography teacher at school had shown them a short film about a girl called Luana whose family had left Syria and ended up in a refugee camp in Uzbekistan, living in a solitary tent with just a few items of their own belongings with them. "This is worse than hell," he remembered the girl saying, "if only people would think of what it is like for us, then perhaps they would be more compassionate." Now here he was standing in a small stone house in Smyrna looking at a family of five trying to get away from the persecution. *It's quite different seeing something on a film and feeling sorry for people compared to actually being presented with the reality of the situation. Perhaps until now I only believed it was important to help refugees; now the reality is that I must do something to help – even if it is just for this family alone.*

"Yes," Ekrem said with a greater tone of confidence in his voice. "I will go and get the supplies you have asked for. It is the least I can do."

"Be careful, Ekrem," said Theophilus. "This task might sound easy, but the risks involved could be tricky."

"What risks?!" Ekrem scoffed. "There's nothing risky about picking up a few groceries..."

"But..." started Theophilus, but Ekrem was already opening the door. One of the family ran to close it quickly behind him. Theophilus looked at the family. "I'm sure he'll be alright," he said, trying to be reassuring. "What he doesn't know about, he won't have to worry about."

*

The temperature of the late afternoon summer sun was much more bearable than it had been earlier when he arrived. Whilst it was still his home country somehow the weather seemed more intense back in the Roman times. *It's probably just my imagination,* he told himself.

Going down into the agora was also not too difficult. *Better to buy both items from the same tradesman, if possible,* he contemplated, *because I don't know the value of these two coins so I can just hand them over and he can give me the change.* There were plenty of people selling bread and plenty of others selling grapes, but none selling both. All around people were finishing their shopping for the day and setting off for home before sunset until there were only a few people left in the agora. The Roman soldiers were around, watching, monitoring and ensuring that there was no trouble.

Ekrem found another trader who was selling both fruit and bread, but there was no sign of any grapes. "I'll buy some bread," he said, picking up the best of the loaves that were left.

"It is durus and sordid," said the trader.

"What does that mean?" asked Ekrem inquisitively. *Sordid normally means horrid or immoral. I don't want to buy anything like that. I want the best for this refugee family.*

"It means that it isn't made with the best flour," replied the trader. "I thought everyone knew that."

"Does it still taste alright?" Ekrem asked, determined to ensure that he wouldn't be making a big mistake.

The man nodded. Ekrem wasn't sure whether the man was bluffing just to make a last sale of the day or whether he was being completely honest. There were no other options for buying any other bread at this time of the day, so he agreed to take it.

"Do you have any grapes?" Ekrem asked.

The tradesman looked most uncomfortable. "I shouldn't be selling them to you," he replied. "I could be risking by business by doing this." He reached down and passed over a blanket inside which was a large bunch of black grapes.

Ekrem handed over the two coins. The trader looked at them, thanked Ekrem very much, and immediately went to packing his remaining goods away. There was no change. Ekrem watched as the tradesman scurried away with his remaining goods, subtly avoiding any Roman soldiers on the way.

I don't know what that was all about, he pondered. *I got the items for the refugee family and that's all that matters.*

*

It was on his way out of the agora that Ekrem got stopped by one of the Roman soldiers who was looking very intently at the bread and the blanket he was carrying.

"What have you got there?" the soldier asked.

"Groceries," replied Ekrem quite calmly, determined to show himself unafraid of this soldier or the one stood behind him.

"Groceries?" asked the soldier. "What are groceries?"

"Food," replied Ekrem, still using his matter-of-fact tone. *They can't deny me buying food, surely?*

The soldier ignored the bread and snatched the blanket out of Ekrem's hand. He unwrapped it and his eyes widened. He nodded to the other Roman soldier who promptly took Ekrem's wrists behind his back and tied them with rope. A second rope was then wrapped around Ekrem's chest and became like a dog lead for the soldier to lead Ekrem away with another one following behind with a spear.

"What are you doing? What is going on?" yelled Ekrem. "Help me, someone!"

"Be quiet!" demanded the soldier with the spear behind him. "Or feel the edge of my spearhead."

This is wrong, Ekrem thought in total disbelief of what was happening to him. *More worryingly though is what's going to happen to me now?*

*

There was no point calling for help or trying to escape. Ekrem was no idiot in realising that both of these things would involve some sort of consequence that he did not want to face. Romans were notorious for hurting, torturing and killing people who had conducted crimes. The only problem was that Ekrem didn't know what he had done wrong. *If only I had listened to Theophilus before leaving the house,* he mused. *Perhaps then I would have been more aware of the risk involved. Note to self: always listen to those who know better than you!*

They eventually reached the Roman centurion's quarters. The end of the rope was tied to another wooden stake whilst the two soldiers went inside to speak to the centurion. Ekrem wondered if he could slip his wrists out of the rope, but there was no escape. As much as he tried, the rope was just cutting into his skin.

"You're trying to escape, I see," said the Roman centurion who had now come out to see him. He was a strong, muscular man with fiery hair and a blazing beard of red. His breastplate and helmet sparkled brightly, and his weaponry sat close to hand. *There's no upsetting this guy,* realised Ekrem. *I don't know what's going to happen here, but I think I'm going to need help.*

"So... you're one of those cannibals, are you?" roared the centurions. "Having one of your love feasts tonight, eh? Well, not anymore you're not." He laughed loudly and contemptuously. "You're a traitor to Rome, but you already know that. Well, for you, it's over. No-one's going to help you now. Take him away!"

The soldiers untied the rope and marched Ekrem across the courtyard to a doorway on the other side. The door opened, behind which were some stone steps spiralling downwards. It was so dark that Ekrem couldn't see how many there were. The soldier pushed him down the first few steps and then slammed the door behind him, locking it, and then leaving him. *This is terrifying! If I try and take any more steps I could slip and fall and break something. It's too dark to see anything! Oh, Theophilus, I'm sorry. Please help...* but his cries sounded like they would hit the ceiling and never escape from this black hole.

*

Theophilus and the refugee family did not take too long to realise that something had happened and that Ekrem was probably in the hands of the Roman soldiers.

"You need to leave," Theophilus told them. "If Ekrem leads the soldiers here, they will find you. Quick, gather your belongings and we will go to the seaport. From there, I will try and get you on a boat to Athens."

The refugee family nodded and quickly huddled themselves together. Theophilus led the way through some of the back streets of the city until they eventually reached the seaport. "Here, get in these," Theophilus instructed, noticing some empty sacks lying on the harbourside close to a ship that was loading for departure. The family looked at him with a look of disgust and unbelief. "It's just until the ship sets sail," Theophilus said. "If you are fortunate, you will be able to hide yourselves on the boat more carefully during the journey; but for now, we must get you on board." Theophilus looked behind him. "Quick, there's a soldier coming." The family clambered into the sacks. Theophilus went over to the sailors and told them that his father had instructed for the sacks to be loaded on board. The sailors nodded.

Before leaving, Theophilus watched from a safe hiding place behind some trees as the sailors lifted the heavy sacks on board the ship. *The family are on board. Now to deal with Ekrem.*

*

The minutes sat on the dark stone steps turned to hours. A number of times Ekrem had managed to stop himself from falling off to sleep, knowing too well that if he fell over, he would risk falling and severely hurting himself. He kept himself busy by thinking about the different places he and Alida had visited, the treasures that he had picked up, and the numerous lessons he had learned on the way. *It's only thanks to Grandpa that I'm in this mess now,* he thought to himself with great levels of self-pity. *Will I ever see my family again? What if they kill me? What happens then?*

Then, without warning, the door just a few steps above him opened and a small chink of light appeared from the moonlit sky.

"Ekrem," hissed a voice. "Are you down there?"

"Theophilus, is that you?" replied Ekrem with a note of joy and optimism in his voice.

"Come on," hissed Theophilus. "Let's get you out of there." Carefully he guided Ekrem step by step out of the black pit and through the wooden door into the courtyard again.

"How did you know where I was?" asked Ekrem.

"That was obvious," replied Theophilus. "When you didn't return, I knew that you had been caught by the Romans."

"But how did you get permission to get me out? And why was it so dangerous to buy bread and grapes? And what's happened to the refugee family? How do we get out of this place? What if someone sees us? Am I ever going to get home again?"

"Questions, questions, questions..." muttered Theophilus. "There isn't time for questions now. Just be quiet and follow me."

Theophilus took the other end of the rope that Ekrem was still attached to and walked confidently towards the courtyard gate that was being guarded by a Roman soldier. The Roman guard got up from his seat.

Uh-oh, thought Ekrem. *Here comes trouble again.* He could imagine both he and Theophilus being taken back to the black pit and thrown to the bottom. Amazingly however, the guard opened up the gate for a chariot that was just arriving. Theophilus just led Ekrem through at exactly the same time in the opposite direction, unnoticed by anyone.

"That was lucky," sighed Ekrem once the gate had closed behind them. "If that chariot hadn't been coming in at the same time, then we would both have been caught for definite."

Theophilus untied the rope from off Ekrem's hands. "Nothing lucky about it," Theophilus said quietly. "I knew that chariot was coming."

"But how?" exclaimed Ekrem. "You couldn't see it and I didn't even hear it."

"I didn't have to hear it or see it," replied Theophilus, "I just knew..."

*

Ekrem's tongue did not say a single word all the way back to the stone house. His mind was simply astounded at how Theophilus knew that the chariot was coming, and he was trying to work out how.

"Listen," said Theophilus. "I have some important questions to ask you, Ekrem. When you were captured by the Romans, what did they accuse you of?"

Ekrem reflected back on the interrogation by the Roman centurion. "I was accused of being a traitor to Rome, being a cannibal, and attending a love feast," he replied.

Theophilus nodded knowingly. "I thought so. It's the bread and grapes that were the problem..."

"But why, Theophilus, why?" begged Ekrem. "I need to know the answer. Did that refugee family set me to get captured or something?"

"No," replied Theophilus. "They are a good family. You got captured because you took a risk, and it went wrong. Listen and I will explain it to you."

For the next hour, Theophilus expounded to Ekrem about how the Romans look to kill rebels, but particularly rebellious Christians. "They know people are Christians when they take bread and wine together. That's what caused the problem with you carrying the bread and the grapes. They naturally assumed that you were going to have bread and wine with some other people."

"Well, I wasn't,' protested Ekrem. "And I don't think that I should have been treated like that. It's an injustice."

"There are many things that are an injustice, Ekrem," Theophilus replied. "You live in a modern world where peoples' rights are considered important, but here in the Roman world, things are not the same. If you are suspected of doing anything different than the Roman way, then you are considered an enemy of Rome."

Ekrem sat back and contemplated over all of these things. His wrists were still sore, but Theophilus treated them with some healing balm. "This has come all the way from Gilead," he said. "This will solve the pain." Ekrem didn't really care where it came from – he was just relieved that the pain and soreness was leaving.

*

The next morning, it was raining. Theophilus explained that he would be departing from Smyrna very shortly. He was apparently going to be helping some more refugees find their way to safer shores than here in Smyrna.

"Here, Ekrem, I want you to take this," he said, holding out two coins in his hand. "Look after them. Treasure them, and don't forget what you have learnt from your experience and time here in Smyrna."

Ekrem looked at the coins. They brought back the memory of the refugee family, the need to buy food, and the significance of the images on the coins themselves.

"Thank you Theophilus," he replied. "I shall – and I will share the lessons from Smyrna with my sister, Alida, as well."

*

Within seconds, Theophilus and the stone house in Smyrna had disappeared and Ekrem found himself back in his living room at home. He crept out of the room and up to his own bedroom, noting that Alida was sound asleep in her room from the faint, but soft snoring tones he could hear. *There will be so much to tell her,* he thought to himself. *I don't think she will be too happy when she finds out that the Romans captured me though.*

He got into his bed and snuggled down under the sheets. One final look at his wrists showed that they had made a complete recovery; and there under the bed, he placed the coins. *Another treasure from Grandpa.* "Thank you, Grandpa," he said, smiling across at the night sky through his bedroom window. "Just out of interest: how did you know all these things?"

*

Chapter 18

The first opportunity that Ekrem had to share with Alida about the things that had happened in Smyrna was after school when their mother sent them down to pick up some necessary groceries from the market down near the Kusadasi harbourside. Despite it being mid-afternoon, the hottest part of the day, the market was still busy with fanatical tourists who, having come off the nearby cruise ships, were buying up souvenirs to take home. It was the usual kind of things – t-shirts with "I love Kusadasi"; bags of tea-beans in various flavours; Turkish spices; Turkish coffee; Turkish delight (the genuine sort); ceramics, leather, keyrings and more. Ekrem and Alida smiled as the coffee seller sold three bags of coffee to a local resident at a lot cheaper price than a German tourist who was trying to barter for a better deal.

"I pay less than this for coffee at home," the German tourist was arguing.

The coffee seller just shrugged his shoulders, and eventually got the asking price he wanted. The tourist left looking unimpressed with the price paid, but secretly pleased to be taking genuine Turkish coffee back home with him.

*

"You ended up where?!" exclaimed Alida. "In prison?!"

"Sssh!" hissed Ekrem, noticing that Alida's statement had caused both amused and bewildered looks from the passers-by. "Look, I was out shopping, like we are now, and I brought some bread and grapes and got arrested by the Romans. But that's not the point. I learnt some really important secrets whilst out there." He proceeded to tell Alida what they were:

1. There is a difference between seeing a situation and getting involved in one.

2. However poor you may be, you still must hold onto hope for a better future.

3. Beware of people who will turn your innocence into guilt, simply because they don't like you.

4. Always do your best for people – never settle for less than the best.

5. Take a stand for that which is right no matter what the opposition may be.

Alida was impressed. *That's certainly some very thoughtful points,* she mused. *Easier said than done, I expect, but important all the same.*

*

Half an hour later, having picked up all the things that their mother had asked them to collect, they made their way home. The long walk up a steep hill from the harbourside to the house where they lived meant that they were extremely tired when they came in the door, bearing two shopping bags each. Ekrem gave his mother the change and both of them went upstairs and collapsed on their beds before dinner.

It wasn't long before they heard their father arrive home. He was humming as he came in the door which seemingly meant he had had a good day. Then a few minutes later came their mother's voice informing them that the dinner was ready. Slowly and steadily, the two tired children came down to the living room. Being so exhausted, they didn't even notice something missing when they came into the living room. It was only as they were taking mouthfuls of 'menemen', a dish made up of eggs and peppers, did Ekrem nearly choke on the food with shock.

"The...the....the....rug!" he spat out. "It's gone. Where is it?"

His mother, whose face had gone quite pale with worry over Ekrem's choking fit, wiped her brow with the napkin. "Don't worry, Ekrem. It's not gone. It's just been sent to be restored."

"But how? Why? When? Where? Who with?" Ekrem spieled out, most anxious about the well-being of the rug.

"Don't panic, Ekrem," his father replied. "You have to admit that the rug needed some attention and restoration. There were even some odd spots of candle wax on it – don't ask me how that got there – and so your mother showed me a card which had been dropped through the front letterbox which offered a paid service to restore the rug. Your mother called the number this morning and they collected it this afternoon. You can see the card if you like."

Ekrem nodded eagerly. His father went to collect the card from the hallway and gave it to Ekrem to read.

"Devrim Carpet and Rug Restoration Services. Telephone: +90 242 424 6791".

"When are they returning the rug?" Alida asked, realising why Ekrem was so agitated.

"They didn't say. I'd imagine about a week. He said it would take time and they would give us a call when it was ready to arrange delivery."

A week! screamed a thought in Ekrem's head. *I can't be waiting a week to visit the final city and discover the last treasure and secrets that Grandpa wanted him to know.*

"Did you have to send it away for restoration now?" Ekrem whined. "Couldn't we get it back and then send it off for restoration in the future?"

His father's face and tone turned from that of being casually relaxed into intense. "Ekrem, I think that's enough talk on the subject. Now please just eat your dinner. I don't want to hear any more of your worries about the rug. It's just a rug."

But's it's not just a rug, Ekrem thought. *It's much more than a rug. If only you knew...*

*

At school the next day, Mehmet was waiting for Ekrem at the gates. "Morning, Ekrem," he said, cheerfully. "How are we?"

Ekrem kept his head down and continued walking, hoping that if he ignored Mehmet for long enough, he might just wander away; but Mehmet was determined to linger.

"I saw your car was away for a night. Did you go anywhere interesting?"

"Izmir," replied Ekrem sullenly. "Yes, it was okay and no, I don't want to tell you anymore about it."

"No need to be unkind, Ekrem. I thought you knew better than that," Mehmet said provokingly. "Not a problem, is there?"

"Well, hopefully, there won't be in a minute," replied Ekrem, hoping that Mehmet would pick up the subtle hint that he wanted to be left alone rather than be aggravated by his annoying neighbour.

"I saw that someone came and collected the rug from your place as well. I can't blame you for getting rid of it," continued Mehmet, "I don't know why you wanted that old thing from your grandfather anyway. Look at all the trouble it caused."

Ekrem was getting more and more annoyed on the inside. He wanted to hit out at Mehmet but realised that he mustn't – firstly because there was never a reason to hit someone (even if they are annoying); and secondly, he would get in trouble.

"I don't want to talk about it!" Ekrem yelled, staring at Mehmet directly in the eyeballs. "Just leave me alone."

"Okay, okay…" replied Mehmet, backing away. "I'll leave you alone." He paused. "I'll go and talk to Alida – she was most helpful last time."

"You leave my sister alone!" yelled Ekrem, but Mehmet was already on his way.

*

That evening, Alida was working on her laptop in her bedroom. She had been busy looking through the internet to try and find the contact details for Devrim Carpet and Rug Restoration Services. *If I find their number, then I can give them a call and see if they can tell me when they will be returning the rug. That will please Ekrem very much.* The internet however was failing to find any business or establishment by that name. She then tried typing in 'Carpet and Rug Restoration' which provided a whole list of people who could do the work, but none of them had the name Devrim. She looked at the card again. It was very frustrating trying to find information and the internet not providing it; but the more she thought about it, the more it dawned on her that their rug was in the hands of someone whose business seemingly didn't exist. Eventually, she tried typing just the words 'Devrim' and 'rug' into the search engine and one result came up. 'Devrim's Auctioneers'.

"Ekrem, Ekrem," she called, dashing down the corridor to his bedroom. He jumped up of his bed and quickly met his sister as she ran into the room. "Ekrem, listen, we have a real problem. The people who came to collect the rug aren't restoring it at all; they're going to auction it!"

Ekrem could hardly believe his ears. He stared at Alida's laptop screen with total disbelief. *What a dreadful trick to play on people,* he thought to himself. *These people turn up to collect peoples' carpets and rugs on the understanding that they are going to be restored; but instead Devrim's staff sell the items at auction and the original owners never see the rug or carpet again.* "We've got to get it back, Alida, before someone else buys it and we never see it again."

Devrim's auction house was about a forty-five-minute cycle ride outside of Izmir. Ekrem and Alida worked out that they could probably go there straight after school the next day and return home before dinner time.

"Alida and I are going to go for a cycle ride after school," Ekrem informed their parents. "We have found out about another site we would like to see which isn't too far from here."

"You be careful," replied their mother. "Ekrem, you are totally responsible for looking after your sister, do you understand?"

Ekrem nodded. He understood all right.

For the entire day, both their minds could focus on nothing else than getting the rug back. *We'll go to the auction house, find the rug and insist that they return it. We'll take a photo of it in the auction house to prove that it was there. Then when we show Father, he can ensure that it does come back.*

As soon as the school day ended, Ekrem and Alida were on their bicycles heading for the auction house. It wasn't easy cycling in the heat of the day, and they were thankful for the bottles of water that they had stashed into their bags from the kitchen that morning.

When they arrived at the auction house, it looked very run-down. The sign was hardly legible and the whole building looked like someone should have demolished it ages ago. The corrugated iron roof was in a very dishevelled place, and anyone passing by in a car would think it was just an abandoned unit with nothing worth having inside. The windows were covered with dirt and cobwebs, so looking inside was quite difficult.

They parked up their bicycles around the side of the building where they wouldn't be seen from the road. "Right," said Ekrem. "Let's find our rug, Alida. Stick right by my side, and if anyone asks, we are just looking around for something interesting to buy. Remember, they don't know who we are."

Alida nodded and followed Ekrem to the old wooden entrance door which creaked terribly as they opened it. The inside of the building was in no ways a reflection of the outside. The place was well organised with hundreds of auction items all over the place from furniture to carpets, ornaments to silver, clothes to paintings, and much more. There was seemingly no-one around, just a sign that read 'ring bell for assistance'. Off to the left-hand side was an office behind some windows. Looking through the glass there was no-one in there either.

"It's terrible to think that a lot of these items may well be stolen," said Alida.

"Well, that's not quite right, Alida," Ekrem whispered back. "You've got to remember that Mother said she paid the man to take it. These people are paying for them to take it away, not realising that they are never going to get it back."

They continued to walk around the main hall. There were plenty of carpets, but no sign of their rug. Off to the far-right hand corner was another small room. "Perhaps it's in there," whispered Alida; but as they turned the corner, a skinny man came heading in the opposite direction, nearly colliding into Ekrem and Alida. It was difficult to know who nearly frightened who. *Clearly, they're not too used to visitors outside of auction times,* thought Ekrem.

"Afternoon," Ekrem greeted the man. "I'm looking for a rug."

The man shrugged his shoulders. Ekrem tried again.

"Have you got any rugs?" he asked politely.

The skinny man simply shrugged his shoulders again and then raised his hands to the side of his face, palms upwards.

"He doesn't understand," said Alida. "Ekrem, have you got a photo of the rug on your phone? You could show it to him."

Ekrem pulled out his mobile and scrolled through the photos. Yes, he did! He turned the screen around for the skinny man to see the picture of the rug. The skinny man's face went red and his whole body stiffened. He shook his head nervously on the spot before scurrying off to the office.

"We had better keep looking," said Ekrem impatiently, looking up and down the smaller room, hoping to catch a glimpse of the rug, but it wasn't there.

*

"He's probably already sold it," moaned Ekrem as he and Alida cycled back home. "We shall never find out the secret of the seventh city – and no-one will ever realise how important that rug is. It will just remain lying on someone's floor until it gets so old that they will burn it and that will be that."

"I'm not so sure," replied Alida. "When you showed that skinny man the photo, he looked quite embarrassed. There's definitely something strange going on…"

*

Chapter 19

With the belief that the rug had been sold, Ekrem was feeling most depressed for the next few days. Alida had tried her hardest to cheer him up, but nothing she had done had made any difference at all. "I'll never know all the secrets," Ekrem kept whining to himself or to Alida when he thought she was listening.

After a while, Ekrem's parents also became concerned about the negative cloud that their son seemed to have come under. They offered to sit down and talk about whatever was troubling him, but Ekrem declined. Eventually one evening at the dinner table, his parents turned to Alida and asked, "Do you know what this is all about?"

Alida was speechless. She didn't want to say 'no' because that would be lying; but if she said 'yes', then the whole story would have to come out. She looked across the table at Ekrem who was manipulating the dinner on his plate with a fork and looking totally miserable. "I don't know if Ekrem wants me to tell you," Alida said, honestly.

Their parents looked at Ekrem who didn't raise his head but continued playing with the food on his plate.

"It's clearly very serious," commented their father, "so I think you'd better tell us, Alida."

Alida took a glimpse at Ekrem who raised his head miserably, looked at his sister, shrugged his shoulders and returned to his original posture.

"Well, it's about the rug," Alida started. "It's not going to be coming back."

"Not coming back? Of course it will come back when they've finished restoring it," replied their mother.

"No, Mother, it won't," continued Alida. "Mr. Devrim is not a carpet and rug restorer. He's an auctioneer. People pay him to take things away for restoration, but instead of restoring things he sells them."

"How do you know all this?" enquired their father.

Alida went on to explain how she and Ekrem had been researching about Devrim and how they had been out to the auctioneers on their bicycles, but there had been no sign of the rug. Her parents looked at her with amazement.

"I shall get onto the police straightaway," said their father, starting to rise from the dinner table.

"You can't," replied Alida. "You've paid them to take the rug away! Don't you understand? It's a scam."

Their father sat himself down again. His two index fingers rested on his bottom lip, his forehead furrowed, and it was clear that he was thinking most carefully about the situation. "Apart from the obvious fact that Ekrem inherited this rug from Grandpa, why is it so important? Surely we could always just buy a new rug."

Ekrem looked up and spoke for the first time that mealtime. His tone was harsh and sad. "We can't," he said. "There's not another rug like that one. It contained secrets and treasures that no-one else knows about."

His parents looked absolutely bewildered. "What do you mean?"

"I'll show you," Ekrem replied, getting up from the table and going to his room. He returned a few minutes later with a number of different items. "These are the treasures that Grandpa wanted me to have."

"Where did they come from?" his mother asked.

"Ephesus, Laodicea, Sardis, Philadelphia, Smyrna, Thyatira... it's a long story," Ekrem said, "and each one of them holds secrets that should never be forgotten."

*

It took another two hours for Ekrem and Alida to share all that happened to them. His parents who initially were quite dubious could only conclude all these things were true. No-one could make up all these kinds of adventures and historical pieces of information. Everyone was so enthralled about it all that they had virtually forgotten about the theft of the rug by the end of it; until Ekrem said, "And that's why the rug is so special, and why I must know the treasure and the secrets of the seventh city."

There was a lengthy period of silence. No-one said anything and no-one moved...

It was interrupted by the ringing of the doorbell. It was Mehmet's mother from across the road.

"I'm so sorry to disturb you," she started. "I hope you weren't doing anything important. It's just that I'm in need of some candles and Mehmet mentioned that you had some in your living room. I was wondering if I could borrow them."

"Why? Yes, of course," said Ekrem's mother, looking quite dubious. "Have you had a power-cut or something?"

"No, no, no, nothing like that... it's just, well... um, yes... well... I'll make sure you get them back," Mehmet's mother answered quite vaguely.

Ekrem's mother went and collected the candles from the living room and handed them over. There was a quick comment from Mehmet's mother about how kind they all were, followed by the closing of the front door again.

"Who was that and what was all that about?" asked Ekrem and Alida's father.

"Oh, that was Mehmet's mother from across the road," their mother replied. "She just wanted to borrow some candles."

"You didn't give her the ones in the living room, did you, Mum?" asked Ekrem.

"Yes," his mother replied. "She's going to bring them back. I think they've got some sort of a problem over there."

Yes, thought Ekrem, *and his name is Mehmet!*

*

Once their parents had gone to bed and were probably asleep, Alida crept into Ekrem's room. They stood gazing out of Ekrem's bedroom window at Mehmet's house. *Well, if Mehmet can spy on us, then it's time we did the same,* Ekrem thought. The Mehmet house was in darkness. Clearly everyone had gone to bed, but then a short while later, a light came on.

"It's probably someone going to the bathroom," said Alida.

The light went off again.

"Told you... wait, look Ekrem, the downstairs light has now come on..."

They both kept watching intently.

"Gone downstairs to get a drink or a midnight snack?" suggested Ekrem.

"It can't be a midnight snack," replied Alida, glancing at the bedroom clock, it's only five minutes past eleven."

"Look!" exclaimed Ekrem, "someone's coming out the side door. It's Mehmet. What's he doing? Quick, Alida, pass me the binoculars from the top shelf."

Alida grabbed the binoculars and handed them to Ekrem. He gazed intently, watching Mehmet's every move.

"He's pumping up his bicycle tires," exclaimed Ekrem. "Why would you do that just after 11pm at night?" Then another thought suddenly struck him "He's going somewhere."

Alida then let out a little shriek which nearly frightened Ekrem stood next to her. She could hardly contain herself. "Ekrem, quickly get some clothes on, we've got to follow him."

"Why?" asked Ekrem, already going across the room and slipping a pair of jeans and a t-shirt over the top of his pyjamas.

"Because..." started Alida. "Mehmet knows where the rug is. Think about it, Ekrem, his mother comes across this evening and asks for the candles. He's probably got those candles in the rucksack on his back. If we stop him now, we'll never know where the rug is, but if we follow him, I think he'll take us to the exact location of the rug. He's planning to visit the seven cities and he knows that he must do this at midnight."

Ekrem looked at his sister with amazement. *She is incredibly clever! Fancy working all that out!* "I think you're right," he said, "come on".

*

Both Ekrem and Alida deliberately kept the front lights of their bicycles off. Although this made cycling in the dark a little more difficult and potentially more dangerous, it was important that Mehmet didn't think he was being followed.

"I know where he's going," hissed Ekrem to Alida after about ten minutes of the journey. "He's going to Devrim's. This is the same route as we went. The rug is there, I bet you."

*

Sure enough, at 11:50pm, Mehmet arrived at Devrim's Auctioneers. He put down his bike outside the front entrance and tiptoed quietly around the side of the building. Little did he know that Ekrem and Alida were close behind him.

"There's Mehmet's bike," said Ekrem. "The rug is definitely here. Now, let's hide our bicycles around the back of the building and find out where Mehmet has gone. Alida, use my mobile to call home and tell Dad and Mum what's happening. Tell them that we shall need their help."

They wheeled their bicycles around the back and Alida started dialling the number for home.

"Once you're done, you keep a lookout for them or for anyone else that might be about. I'm going after Mehmet," said an incredibly determined Ekrem.

*

It took a few minutes for Ekrem to find the door left partly ajar that Mehmet had used to enter the building. Inside it was all dark. Ekrem knew that he had his torch in his pocket, but he didn't want to use it in case he brought attention to himself. At the same time, he would need to go very cautiously – knocking something over or tripping over something would certainly cause a problem – no, it had to be one gradual step at a time. Then he heard a noise of something below him that had fallen over. *It's coming from under the floor,* thought Ekrem curiously. *There must be an underground room. I bet that's where Mehmet is. Now I must find the stairs to get down there.* He continued creeping through the darkness, looking for the stairs without being heard.

*

Alida was stood outside keeping watch. It was quite terrifying standing alone in the darkness. *I hope Ekrem finds Mehmet quickly so we can get out of here.* She couldn't quite imagine what the encounter between Ekrem and Mehmet would involve, but she knew that Mehmet would absolutely hate and deny everything he was up to.

It was as she was pondering over these thoughts that she spotted car lights coming in the distance. *Just a passing car, I guess.* She tucked herself back a little to keep out of the glare of the headlights, but to her horror, the car pulled up outside of the building. *I'd better find Ekrem quickly before anything happens to him.* She found the doorway through which Ekrem had entered the building and was tiptoeing as quickly and as quietly as she could. "Ekrem," she hissed into the blackness. "We've got to get out of here. Ekrem!" There was no reply. She carried on through the darkness of the auction room until there was a little light coming from the illumination of the moon shining in through a nearby window. "Ekrem," she whispered again, but there was still no reply. She gazed out of the window and saw the driver of the car getting out of his vehicle. "There's someone here!"

*

Back at their home, Ekrem and Alida's parents couldn't believe that someone would phone them at minutes to midnight. Their father staggered out of bed and down the hallway to the phone. *Whoever calls people at this time of night needs their head tested,* he thought to himself, before repenting of his negative response, realising that maybe someone had an emergency and needed their help. He couldn't believe it when he heard Alida's voice at the other end of the phone.

"Father, it's me, you need to get to Devrim's Auctioneers straight away. We think we've found the rug, but there could be some trouble, so we need your help."

"But why aren't you in bed?" replied her father, being only half-awake and not realising the seriousness of the situation.

"There's no time to explain," replied Alida. "We need you quickly!" The phone rang off.

Their father dashed into the bedroom, flicking the main light on and starting to throw on a coat, a pair of socks and a set of shoes.

"What are you doing?" cried his wife, realising that something urgent was happening.

"Getting Ekrem, Alida and the rug back from a dubious auctioneer," he replied. "That's where they are now!"

"Then I'm coming too!" replied his wife. "Pass me the car keys. Let's go!".

He looked at his wife. She wasn't even going to bother putting clothes or shoes on. She simply grabbed the keys and was already halfway down the stairs. *She's a gutsy woman,* he thought to himself. *Now let's go and rescue our children.*

*

Mehmet had finished completing the layout of the rug. All seven candles were in position, and he was poised with matches in his hand, ready to light the candles. *This is it! Now this rug and all its secrets and treasures are mine. Ekrem will have no idea where his rug has gone, and I will find out everything he knows and more.* He was about to light the candles, but accidently knocked one over and it made a noise as it rolled across the floor and bumped into the nearby wall. Mehmet froze, waiting for the candle to stop moving. He listened carefully. *No...no noise.* He tiptoed across and picked it up, replacing it back into position. He struck the match and lit the first three candles. Then came a sound from upstairs. He quickly blew out the match. *Did something upstairs fall over? Maybe just the draught through the old window frames.* He listened intently again. Nothing.

Once all seven candles were lit, Mehmet put the matches down and stood next to the one with the letter 'T'. He was about to pick up the candle when an unexpected voice came from behind him.

"It's not going to work, Mehmet," Ekrem said confidently.

"Ekrem!" exclaimed Mehmet. "What are you doing here? How did you find out?" He quickly picked up the candle with the letter 'T' on it, but nothing happened.

"I told you it's not going to work," repeated Ekrem, walking closer and closer towards Mehmet.

Mehmet panicked and rushed across to pick up the candle with the letter 'E' on it. Once again, nothing happened.

"See, I told you," said Ekrem, grabbing Mehmet around the neck and pushing him up against the wall. He was about to hit him with the other hand when he heard a ringing noise coming from upstairs. "Quick," he yelled to Mehmet. "We've got to go."

*

The lights of the whole building suddenly came on as two men arrived through a door in the wall opposite the window. One of the men was the skinny man that they had seen the other day; whilst the shorter man looked more official even if he was a little tired and grumpy. *That's probably Mr. Devrim,* Alida thought to herself. She hid herself under a table draped over by an antique cloth so as to not be spotted by the men when they would come around the corner. *I need to let Ekrem know about the danger he's in and distract the men from finding him.* An idea then came into her brain. She took the mobile phone out of her pocket, found the number for Devrim's Auctioneers and called it. The phone in the office rang. *Hopefully Ekrem will hear it,* she thought to herself.

The two men dashed into the office and picked up the phone. Alida could hear them saying, "Hello, hello, who is this?" and other such words down the end of the phone.

The sound of footsteps came from a set of stairs and from her view from under the table, Alida could see Ekrem appear on the shop floor followed closely behind by Mehmet.

The two men had also heard the footsteps and came out of the office. "Kids!" said the skinny man.

"Who are you?" shouted the shorter man, pointing at Ekrem. "And what are you doing here?" he continued, pointing at Mehmet.

*

Whilst the two men escorted Ekrem and Mehmet into the office, Alida crept out from her hiding place under the table and nearly got out of the door when she felt a strong pair of arms pick her up by her waist and carry her out the door before putting her down again.

"Father!" she cried. "You made it. Thank you!"

"Now you go and join your mother in the car," instructed her father. "I will go and get Ekrem."

"He's in the office with Mehmet and two other men. One of them is Mr. Devrim, I think," Alida called as she watched her father go disappearing off down the side of the building.

*

"Devrim! Come out!" yelled Ekrem's father as he re-entered the building. The two men in the office nearly jumped out of their skin and went flying out of the office as quickly as possible followed closely behind by Ekrem and Mehmet.

"Who are you?" demanded Mr. Devrim. "What do you want at this time of night?"

"That boy there," Ekrem's father started, pointing at Ekrem, "is my son and I have to come to collect him and the rug which belongs to us and take them home."

"What are you talking about?" questioned Mr. Devrim. "Why is your son even here in the first place? And which rug are you talking about? We have many here."

"I think I will answer that," started Ekrem before his father could continue. "This boy, Mehmet, lives opposite us and he was leaving the house at about 11pm tonight on his bicycle. I figured that he was up to mischief, so I decided to follow him. He arrived here and entered this building. I wanted to see what he was up to."

"And what was he doing?" enquired Mr. Devrim, still looking at Ekrem seriously and occasionally glaring at Mehmet quite severely.

"Well, I think he's trying to set alight one of your rugs," Ekrem bluffed. "If you go down into your basement, you'll see that he's got a number of candles burning away on top of a rug. If you're not careful the flames could end up going out of control and setting fire to the whole establishment."

Good one, admired Ekrem's father. *I couldn't have thought of a better way to put it myself.*

Mehmet glared at Ekrem. He was about to contradict the statement but couldn't think of a plausible explanation to offer. Mr. Devrim charged down the stairs closely followed by Berkay. He returned a few minutes later, moping his brow.

"No damage done," he sighed. "The candles are all out. I don't even know where the candles came from."

"Our house," replied Ekrem's father, "and the rug for that matter. I believe that you charged my wife to restore it."

"Ah, well, yes…" stuttered Mr. Devrim. "I haven't had a chance to do it yet…"

"Well, I think I will take the rug and the candles back now if you don't mind, with a full refund as well; and Ekrem and I will leave you to deal with your real culprit here."

Mr. Devrim nodded his head most agreeably and fetched the money from the office whilst Ekrem and his father went to collect the rug and the candles.

"But Uncle…" whined Mehmet, "I wanted to…"

"Uncle?!" exclaimed both Ekrem and his father.

*

Chapter 20

"What happened with Mr. Devrim?" asked Alida in the car on the way back home.

Ekrem and his father spent the entire journey (and another hour at home) recalling what had happened and why.

"So, Mehmet, knowing that his uncle refurbished carpets mentioned to Mr. Devrim that there was a rug in our house that would probably need restoring?"

"Yes," replied Ekrem. "Mr Devrim drops the card in the door whilst we were away in Izmir and Mum then contacts him to collect the rug. Mehmet worked out by my reaction at school that the rug had gone to his uncle's auction house. All he needed now were the candles."

"So, he asks his mum to get the candles, puts them in his rucksack bag and sets off to arrive at his uncle's shop in time to light the candles at midnight and go on a journey. In the meantime, he hopes that you will believe the rug has been sold and give up on the whole matter," continued Alida, connecting all the pieces together in her brain.

"Exactly," replied Ekrem.

"Just one thing I don't understand," Alida continued, "you said that you told Mehmet that it wouldn't work when he picked up the candles. How could you be so certain?"

"Mehmet didn't know which places we had already been to. The candles only work once so as long as he kept on picking up candles of places we had been, he wouldn't be going anywhere. The only candle I knew he mustn't pick up was the one marked with the letter 'P' so I deliberately stood right near that one so he wouldn't come near it."

Smart, thought Alida, *very smart!* She felt immensely proud of her big brother.

*

The next morning, whilst Ekrem and Alida were at school, there was knock on the front door of their house. Their mother went to answer it. Stood outside was Berkay holding an envelope in one hand and a bucket with various materials in the other. Their mother took the envelope and read it:

Dear Madam,

Please accept my humble apologies for the misunderstanding over the restoration of your rug. I have sent my associate over to your home today to restore your rug for you with our compliments at no cost to yourselves in return for the inconvenience caused. Normally we would not clean rugs within homes but hope that you will accept this one-off occasion.

Yours kindly

Mr. Devrim

p.s. I have spoken with Mehmet's parents and together we will be ensuring that no further trouble to yourselves is caused.

She smiled and let Berkay into the living room where he got to restore the rug for the rest of the day.

"I thought they were only an auction house," said their father that evening. "Like Ekrem and Alida, I thought they were stealing peoples' things."

"No, that's where we got things wrong," answered their mother. "I placed a phone call with Mr. Devrim today thanking him for his note and services. It seems that he also does do carpet and rug restoration in the basement of his auction house. That's why that area is sealed off from the public when they come to visit."

"And that's why we couldn't see the rug the first time we visited," added Ekrem, feeling pleased with himself.

"I think I've learnt some important lessons from all of this," Alida chipped in.

1. You should never misjudge people. Find out the truth before you make any judgements.

2. Those who wish harm will steal, kill or even destroy anything to get their own way.

3. Think before you agree to anything. Check out the information before you go ahead.

4. Beware of aggravating people like Mehmet.

"Good thoughts, Alida," replied her mother. "I wish all children would think as deeply and as carefully as you do. Perhaps you could help them one day."

Alida nodded. "Perhaps I will. Maybe thoughts like these might then stick in their minds for when they face challenging situations."

"Speaking of Mehmet," interrupted Ekrem, "he wasn't at school today. Do you think he's alright?"

"I'm sure he's fine," replied their mother. "Now, an early night for you two tonight. You've got a busy night ahead I think..."

Ekrem and Alida looked at each other. "Yes, we think we have," they chortled.

*

Alida and Ekrem had both set their alarm clocks for 11:50pm. Neither of them were prepared to miss the final trip to the seventh city. They crept out of their bedrooms and followed each other downstairs and to the living room door. They gently pushed it back and crept into the darkness of the room. Ekrem had just closed the door very quietly when the living room lights suddenly came on.

"Surprise!" came two grown-up voices. Father and Mother had been sat in the darkness waiting for them to arrive. On the side table were four empty mugs and a plate of Turkish delight. The newly refurbished rug was looking spectacular, and the candles were already set out on their saucers on the rug. Father was already holding the matches in his hand.

"What are you doing down here?" asked Alida.

"We had to come down and see for ourselves," replied their father. "As you'll only be gone for about five minutes, we thought we would have some Turkish delight and some tea when you come back."

"Why don't you come with us?" Ekrem asked his parents. "I am sure that if Mother held Alida's hand and Father held my hand then we could all go."

"No, no, no, no, no..." exclaimed their father. "You're not getting your mother or I to leave this warm, comfortable sofa. No, we'll wait for you, and you can tell us all about it when you come back."

Once the candles were all lit, Ekrem and Alida went and stood either side of the candle marked with the letter 'P'.

"Well, this is it," Ekrem said. "Come on, Alida, let's go." Together they picked up the candle and the living room went dark, and everything disappeared.

*

Alida found herself standing behind a large group of English-speaking tourists who were queuing to go on a cable car up to the top of a very insanely steep incline. The man with the white hair and the bald patch in the middle nearly jumped out of his skin when a twelve-year-old girl appeared from seemingly out of nowhere. The cable car arrived and everyone, including Alida, clambered on board. *I have no idea where I am,* she thought, *but for the moment I will just follow the crowd. I am bound to find out soon.* Sure enough, the cable car reached the top and everyone got out to an enormous site of ruins. *That's more like it,* thought Alida. *This is the kind of place I would have expected.*

The man at the front of the crowd was apparently a tour guide. He started talking in English about the site and its history. *Good thing I understand English,* Alida thought. *I am already learning lots.*

189

The site was apparently called Pergamum and was situated close to Bergama. It had originally been the capital city of Attalus the First, close to 200BC. When his grandson, Attalus the Third, became ruler, he handed the city back to the Roman Empire.

All around her, Alida could see long indoor tunnels, paved streets with broken columns, a Hellenistic amphitheatre which was one of the steepest around, holding nearly ten thousand people.

The city once boasted of an impressive library that held approximately two thousand books, it's remains still evident to this day. *This is a very impressive city,* pondered Alida. As she continued walking, she noticed that there were ruined remains of temples everywhere – one to Zeus under which was written the words 'king of kings'; another to Dionysus where much wine was drunk and the dancing and partying was so full-on that people could even drop dead from exhaustion; another one to Demeter who was believed to provide the people with food; another to Athena, the goddess of wisdom; and yet another to the emperor Trajan who offered peace and identity to all who acknowledged him as a god in Pergamum.

Further down the street was a statue of a Roman governor holding a sword. The information read that this was the 'Roman sword', a sign of authority for life and death. *So, if you followed the Roman way of life, you were fine, but if you rebelled, then you were killed,* considered Alida, noticing that there was a stone recalling a man called Antipas, who had been Bishop of Pergamum, and ended his life being killed inside a brazen bull-shaped altar that was used for getting rid of evil.

There was a tap on Alida's shoulder. Alida swung around, expecting to see the old man or the tour guide whom she had been with earlier.

"Remember me?" came a girl's voice.

"Kayra! It's so good to see you again," Alida greeted her. The two girls hugged, and fist punched each other.

"So, what do you think of this place, eh?" asked Kayra. "Stunning views, aren't they?"

"They certainly are," Alida replied. "I can honestly say that I have never been here before and I don't think my parents have either, but they would find it very intriguing. I will have to bring them here."

"Come with me," beckoned Kayra, "and I will give you something incredibly special to keep." Kayra led Alida away from the main part of the site and across to a small grassy area overlooking the landscape below.

191

Down on her hands and knees, Kayra started rummaging through the grass. "Come and join me, Alida," she beckoned.

"But what are we looking for?" asked Alida.

"Small white stones – not the chalky sort that are often lying around, but marble ones that are about the same size as your little finger."

Both girls kept searching and searching. Eventually Kayra found one.

"Like this," she called to Alida, holding up the white stone to the light. It glimmered from the light of the sun and looked absolutely beautiful.

"Have you got one yet?" Kayra called to Alida a short while later.

"I've found two," Alida responded, "but I want to find two more."

Eventually, with some help from Kayra, Alida had four white marble stones in her hand. Kayra also had her own one in her hand. They looked absolutely gorgeous.

"Beautiful stones for beautiful people," commented Kayra. "In the Ancient World these stones were used by the emperor to invite people to meet with him or attend an event that he was hosting. The emperor would write the name of the person invited on the white marble stone and send it to them. If therefore, you received one of these, then you were received as a faithful friend to the emperor."

Alida looked down at her four white stones. *Wow, whoever would have thought that this is what these stones were for – both an invitation and an acceptance from the emperor.*

"Why did you want four?" asked Kayra.

"That's obvious," said Alida, "one for my father, one for my mother, one for Ekrem and one for myself. When I get home, I shall write their names on these stones with my permanent marker and give them to them. I know, my brother, Ekrem, would be most pleased, particularly as they've come all the way from Pergamum."

After half an hour of admiring the scenery, the girls got up to go. The cable car was scheduled to arrive and Alida found herself back with the original group she had arrived with. There was a young man fiddling with his camera, and the older man was sitting on a large stone resting his weary feet. The rest of the crowd were busily chatting away. One lady said to another, "No souvenirs to take away from here then."

"No," replied the other. "Well, you wouldn't expect there to be, would you?"

Alida smiled to herself. *Well, I've got a souvenir to take away – four in fact.* She turned to tell Kayra about what the lady had said, but Kayra had once again disappeared.

*

Chapter 21

Ekrem found himself standing inside a rather large stone building which had a very poignant and pungent smell about the place. It was unpleasant and made Ekrem initially feel sick until he became acquainted with. *Where am I?* he thought to himself, looking around the room. There was a large stone table in the centre, benches across to the side and another smaller table holding bottles of unknown mixtures inside and some rather unpleasant, sharp-looking knives with very intricate blades.

"Ah ha," said the voice of a quirky man who had entered into the room from the door to the side of Ekrem. He was thin, shrivelled and had very bony fingers. He wore a strange looking leather belt that had things hanging off of it by bits of rope. "My new assistant has arrived." The man's eyes looked up to the ceiling and his lips uttered a prayer, but not loud enough for Ekrem to make out the words. On his finger, the man wore a ring with some Roman letters inscribed on it – IC, XC, NI, KA.

New assistant? questioned Ekrem. *I don't see any new assistant.*

The quirky man came over to Ekrem and slapped him so hard on the back that Ekrem nearly fell over. "Welcome, my new assistant, my name is Basilius – I have been waiting for a decent helper for a long time. Have you been to a medical centre before?"

Ekrem's mind quickly flashed back to the medical centre that he and his family were registered with back in Kusadasi.

"Yes, I've been to a medical centre before," replied Ekrem, gazing intently at Basilica. "They did an excellent job at making me better."

"Well, this is my medical centre," Basilica continued. "It's known as the Asklepion Healing Centre here in Pergamum, and quite honestly, I am the best doctor in the whole of the city. People travel from miles, sometimes even other countries, to be treated here in this centre. I am sure you noticed the queue when you came in."

No, I didn't, Ekrem reflected. *I didn't even come in the door. I just arrived here.*

"Your duties are fairly obvious – just get anything I ask for, watch and learn," continued Basilica. "You can manage that, I am sure."

Ekrem nodded. It didn't sound too difficult, did it? *I mean, getting things for him and watching wasn't going to be too strenuous. Besides, it might help with some Science experiment at school one day.*

"What kind of treatments do you do here?" asked Ekrem, eager to hear about the medical options available.

"Oh, that's easy," replied Basilica, looking quite pleased with himself. "Most of our patients actually stay here for a few days or weeks before their treatment to help them become relaxed and calm in mind and body. Then most people have their treatment using hot and cold mud baths, surgeries, use of herbal treatments, special foods, that sort of thing. We shall be starting shortly."

*

Within a couple of hours, Ekrem had witnessed a number of people come in and receive different treatments. Some of them had reported to feel much better afterwards, and in many respects Basilica himself was being treated much like a god. Ekrem too felt quite honoured to be working alongside him until two people arrived who received an extremely negative response from Basilica.

The first was a woman who was about to give birth to her first child. She was clearly in a lot of pain, but Basilica refused her any medical assistance. The second was a very frail man in his elderly years who could barely move or walk. He had been brought to the centre by his son, but again, Basilica refused to treat the poor, old man.

"We don't deal with anyone that might die," Basilica told Ekrem when he challenged him about the need to help everyone in the community with a heart of love and compassion. "It doesn't do my reputation any good if people die. My business will suffer if people think they might die. No, Ekrem, this business is all about health and wealth."

"But is health and wealth everything?" questioned Ekrem.

"Here in Pergamum, it is. Everything in this city is about health and wealth. We go to the Roman temples to receive our provision, favour from the gods, healing, wisdom, everything that we need. That's what religion is for here in Pergamum – health and wealth."

"But what about compassion for the poor? What about those who are suffering? What about weeping with those who are weeping and rejoicing with those who are rejoicing? These are the values that I am taught about at school", argued Ekrem.

"Huh!" replied Basilica, turning his back on Ekrem. "We will talk about this later. Just remember that when you are sick and ill one day, it's me that you will be coming to."

Well, actually, it won't be, thought Ekrem. *Now-a-days the doctors and nurses that we have in our hospitals work out of compassion and care for all people; and I am most thankful for that. Perhaps not thankful enough.*

The last patient of the day looked particularly ill. Ekrem, by now, was feeling tired. He had become quite acquainted with the different remedies that Basilica had been using, but nothing prepared him for what was coming next.

"Ekrem, go and fetch the incense," Basilica instructed him firmly. "It's the gold coloured one in the last jar by the outer door."

Ekrem went to find it and returned with the jar. When Basilica opened it, a pungent fragrance filled the air, but it was not pleasant. It smelt musky, dry and foul. Basilica took some of the fragrance and started to put the patient into a trance. *This is really weird,* thought Ekrem, *I know they don't have anaesthetics, but this is seriously strange.*

Basilica left the room for a few moments. The patient certainly did seem to be going into a deep sleep-like state. When Basilica did come back, he was carrying some snakes that hissed and slithered around in his arms. Each one was over a metre long and Basilica was bringing in three of them! Ekrem, who didn't like snakes, nearly freaked out! He wanted to leave the room as quickly as possible but was also resilient to hold his position to see what would happen next. Basilica laid the snakes over the patient's body and let them slither all over him.

"What are you doing?" Ekrem murmured to Basilica, horrified to see the sight of the snakes crawling and hissing over the patient's body.

"The snake skin's oil will help to cure this patient. By letting the snake run over his body, the oil will enter into the pores of the skin and bring about the healing that he will need. After this, I will bring in the sacred dogs from the temple who will lick his body clean and then he will be completely recovered," Basilica informed Ekrem. "I have done this treatment many times before."

"That's disgusting!" Ekrem exclaimed. "And... and... and... the poor patient doesn't even know what is happening to him."

"Do you think he would let me do this treatment if he did?" asked Basilica. "Now, Ekrem, switch out the lights and close the door. We'll come back and finish the treatment later.

*

Ekrem couldn't sleep that night for the nightmares he kept having about the snakes. He woke up a few times in quite a sweat.

"I can't stay here," he said to himself. "I must leave and hide myself somewhere." *But where do I go? I don't know anything else about this city that I am in.*

His mind eventually concluded that he had but two choices: the first was to stay and continue to work with Basilica; the second was to leave and see if there was somewhere else that he could stay in the city. The second choice seemed best. He got himself up, crept out of the building and set off in the darkness of the night to another part of the city.

*

It wasn't long before he noticed that someone had drawn a fish sign in the dust outside of the front door of a stone house. His mind flashed back to his time in Smyrna. *I remember what this symbol is for, even if the Romans don't,* Ekrem thought to himself. He knocked on the door. After a few minutes, the door opened steadily and Ekrem was admitted in.

Somehow Ekrem had been expecting a modest home, much like the one he had visited last time, but this one was different. It was a two roomed house, one kitchen and one living room. There were a group of men sat around on the floor staring at some kind of statue at the front of the room. Ekrem decided to sit right at the back, close to the door where he had entered, and keep himself conspicuous. He watched as some women brought forth meat, probably lamb, from the kitchen and laid it in front of the statue before returning to the kitchen. Then all the men in the room started saying some kind of chant which Ekrem didn't understand.

"They're offering meat to idols," said a voice from next to him.

Ekrem turned. Theophilus was sat right next to him.

"Theophilus, where did you suddenly come from?" Ekrem asked, astonished that Theophilus was in the room. He certainly hadn't noticed him when he had arrived.

"I saw you were here," replied Theophilus, "so I thought I would join you. I won't be staying long though. I refuse to be part of this crowd, but for your sake, I will stay a short while so that you understand."

*

After quite a time, the men had finished eating and drinking. Ekrem had felt quite hungry himself and had asked Theophilus if he could get some of the meat himself. Theophilus had told him he couldn't and passed him a piece of bread that he had been carrying in his bag. It wasn't as half as tasty as the meat had looked, but Ekrem thanked Theophilus for his generosity.

"Right, it's time to leave," Theophilus said. "You're coming too, Ekrem."

Ekrem was too tired to argue or to question why. He simply followed Theophilus who opened the front door and they both slipped out into the night air again.

"Is that it?" asked Ekrem, wondering if anything else would be happening that night.

"It is for us," said Theophilus. "As for the men in the house we've just left, they will be partying for quite some time tonight once more of their guests have arrived."

Ekrem told Theophilus that he was too tired for a party anyway. "One thing that does confuse me though," continued Ekrem, "is the symbol of that fish that was outside the door. When we were in Smyrna, you told me that the people who drew that symbol were good people and faithful to their non-Roman beliefs, but back there, they were offering food to a Roman statue."

"You have observed well," said Theophilus. "These people have mixed their beliefs with the culture around them. They think that it is too difficult to do anything different; so, they follow their beliefs, and they behave as the Romans would want them to, even if it means compromising a little here and there."

*

Ekrem thought hard about what he had witnessed here in Pergamum. *What secrets have I learnt here?*

1. The importance of treating all people as equal.

2. The need to help the sick, the dying, those in pain.

3. Health and wealth are essential, but there are other important things as well, including love, compassion, friendship, hope and purpose.

4. Compromising is not always right, particularly if it involves doing something wrong.

A sudden jolt happened in his mind. "Theophilus," he started. "This is the seventh city, which means this is it.

I've finished finding the secrets of the seven cities that Grandpa wanted me to discover. You haven't led me to, or given me, a treasure for this place yet, and I don't know if I will ever see you again..."

But Theophilus had disappeared.

*

Back in the living room, Ekrem and Alida's parents were eagerly awaiting their return, still sat in darkness. They didn't want to put the lights back on in case that created some kind of problem, and also, they were curious to see whether the candles would automatically re-light themselves when Ekrem and Alida came back.

"Hello," came the first voice in the darkness. "Are you still there?"

"Yes, Alida, we're here," replied her father. "We're just waiting for Ekrem."

"I'm here," answered Ekrem, having just arrived when his father was speaking.

The lights of the living room were turned back on, and the family sat down together on the sofas. For a moment, no-one spoke. Ekrem was exhausted from his visit and Alida was still contemplating about the stones she held in her hand.

"Well, what happened?" asked their parents. "Did you both go together?"

"No," replied Ekrem. "Dad, Mum, it was horrible. There was this freaky man who was using snakes to make people better. I thought I was going to die..."

"Whereas I had a most interesting visit with a tour group," Alida interrupted, "and learnt lots of interesting things about Pergamum as well as seeing the most spectacular views and having a cable car ride. Oh, we must go there one day – all of us."

"I didn't see any views," moaned Ekrem, "it was night-time when I was in the city and there were some very strange people around."

Their mother fetched some tea and their father passed around the Turkish delight. It felt quite unusual sitting around the living room at midnight drinking tea and eating Turkish delight, but in many ways, Ekrem saw it as a commemoration of Grandpa's legacy – the seven cities had been visited, the secrets of the cities were known, and the treasures...

"Oh, there's only six treasures. I never got a treasure from the seventh city. Somehow, I must have missed it," uttered Ekrem.

"No, you didn't," smiled Alida. "I have the treasure from the seventh city, but I will need to give it to you in a moment." She dashed out the room and up the stairs. A few minutes later, she returned into the room and handed out the white marble stones, each with the person's name on it. "Here, Ekrem, this is yours," she said.

Ekrem took the white marble stone and looked at it. "This is a beautiful stone," he said, "but what does it mean?"

"It means you're accepted," said Alida, "and if a Roman emperor had dropped it off to you right now, you'd be invited to dine with him."

Awesome, thought Ekrem, *this is probably the best treasure yet.*

*

Once all the tea had been consumed and the majority of the Turkish delight eaten, the whole family started to head upstairs for the night.

"Oh well," sighed Ekrem, "no more adventures to interesting and exciting places for a little while now then..."

"Don't be so hasty," said his father. "I think I have one more special place in mind."

"Really?" Ekrem answered.

"Just you two be up early again in the morning..." he smiled. "You'll see..."

*

Chapter 22

Despite being exhausted from a really late bedtime the night before, Ekrem and Alida were up early the next morning. Father had said something about going to a special place and both of them were keen to know where. Whilst waiting, they were both speculating about where it could be.

"I bet that he's taking us to Miletus," said Ekrem. "That's a famous set of ruins too with some interesting history about it. I was looking it up on my I-pad this morning."

"I don't think we shall be going to see any more ruins," answered Alida. "I know that we have been going on all these adventures, but Father wouldn't want to 'ruin' today by seeing more old stones and pillars, would he?" she laughed.

"Perhaps he's taking us to the animal park in Izmir. You know how much he wanted to go there last time."

"Or maybe he's taking us to Istanbul to do some more shopping and see the sites there," suggested Alida.

Their father stuck his head around the living room door. "You're both wrong so far," he said, chuckling to himself.

He disappeared out the room and through the front door to check that the car was ready.

"I know," said Ekrem, an idea suddenly jumping into his head. "Let's go and check out the boot of the car and see if there are any suitcases or other clues inside."

They both dashed out to the car and whilst their father was filling the windscreen wash container in the bonnet, they opened the boot. There was nothing inside. Ekrem and Alida sighed. "Then I have no idea," said Ekrem. "I guess we shall have to wait until we get there."

Their father called through the front door, "time to go" and he and the two children climbed in the car. Their mother came out the house last, carrying a rather large rucksack on her back. It was the sort that someone would normally use when they go backpacking. Ekrem and Alida eyed it up suspiciously. *We can't be going backpacking,* thought Ekrem. *She's only got one bag.*

*

"The journey is going to be a long one," announced their father as they started off. "That's why we've had to leave early. It's going to be about three hours."

"Three hours!" exclaimed Ekrem and Alida. "That's ages."

And it certainly was. Father had taken the E87 road which went via Aydin and Nazilli in the direction of Denizli.

"We're remarkably close to the first city you visited - Laodicea," their father informed the family, "but that's not where we're going."

They travelled on a little further past Denizli. Ekrem and Alida were busy watching the clock and then gazing out the window. Father had said it was about three hours and time was nearly up. They had to be there by now, surely.

Then all of a sudden, Ekrem and Alida could see it. It looked like a snowy landscape that ought to have a castle on the top.

"Wow, look at that snow!" exclaimed Ekrem.

"That's not snow," replied his father. "That's cotton."

"No way!" replied Ekrem. "You mean, that landscape is all cotton."

"Yes," replied his father, "the place is called Pamukkale and that's exactly where we're going; but that's not the best part of it."

The level of excitement in the car rocketed from 'high' to 'through the roof'. There was cheering and clapping, including from Father who took his hands off the wheel for just a few seconds or so.

On arrival, the children were just in awe of all that was around them. First, their parents took them to see the cotton landscape which stretched as far as the eye could see. The minerals within the ground had caused a cotton landscape to develop with many large, thermal pools of water all over the place.

"You can walk all over here," said their father. "Come on, let's go."

The walk was spectacular. All around everything was white and yet the warm summer sun shining on their arms and legs made them feel anything but cold or wintry. It was surely a fairy tale environment with such beauty, calm and relaxation.

They all slipped their sandals off, and their mother was the first to get into the hot, thermal waters. Ekrem and Alida were close behind and finally their father.

"This water is so beautiful," exclaimed Alida.

"What's the secret behind this water, Father?" asked Ekrem.

Ekrem's father went onto explain about how these were thermal waters that were used for bringing healing about to people who had rheumatic or arthritic conditions and perhaps other ailments as well.

"I remember now," Ekrem said, "these are the hot waters that would flow down towards Laodicea. Yes, people used to get some level of healing here – certainly better than having to go to the medical centre in Pergamum."

*

After a long time of walking, the family were heading back to the car. "That was wonderful," said Alida.

"Yes, thank you for bringing us to this fantastic place," added Ekrem. "I think Grandpa would have loved it here."

"Haven't you forgotten something?" said their mother.

"What?" answered Ekrem, looking puzzled.

"My large rucksack in the car?" answered his mother.

It's got a picnic lunch inside, Ekrem thought to himself excitedly, *we're going to have a picnic, I'm sure.*

His father opened the boot and lifted out the heavy rucksack. He put it down on the ground and both Ekrem and Alida opened it as fast as they could. "Towels," they said, pulling them out from the bag. "Swimming costumes!" they yelled with great excitement.

"Come on, follow me," said their father.

With their mother following closely behind, their father, carrying the heavy rucksack, led the way around to the pool of Cleopatra, a type of large swimming pool of hot thermal waters surrounded by beautiful trees and plants. It was the most exciting swimming pool that the children had ever seen in their lives.

"The changing area is over there," their father pointed out to them. "Now you two go and get changed and leave your mother and I to have some peace for a while."

Ekrem and Alida darted off to their retrospective changing areas and returned shortly. Climbing into the pool, their hearts were overwhelmed with happiness and joy. The waters were just so incredibly amazing and swimming in them was phenomenal. Their parents watched their two young people jumping, diving, swimming, laughing and shouting.

"I'm just so proud of them both," said their father, reflecting over all that his two young people had discovered and learnt from their adventures.

Their mother nodded. "Come on," she said. "Let's leave them to enjoy themselves for a while."

*

Ekrem and Alida spent so much time swimming in the water that they both exhausted themselves out. Ekrem had got out of the water and was sitting in the shade of one of the trees. Alida had stayed in the water relaxing and kicking her feet, watching the ripples drift across the water.

"Do you come here often?" asked a girl next to her.

"No, this is my first time here," answered Alida, continuing to stare at the ripples and not looking at the person who spoke to her.

"Do you come here often?" asked a boy standing quite close to where Ekrem was sitting in the shade of a tree.

"No, this is my first time," replied Ekrem, not turning to look at the person who was speaking.

"Alida…" said the girl's voice.

"Ekrem…" said the boy's voice.

"Kayra!" cried Alida. "You're here! You've got to meet my brother!"

"Theophilus!" cried Ekrem. "You're here! You've got to meet my sister, Alida!"

He and Theophilus rushed back to the pool and found Alida with Kayra.

"Ekrem, meet Kayra," shouted Alida, jumping up and down with excitement.

"Alida, meet Theophilus," yelled Ekrem, jumping into the pool with an enormous splash.

Everyone hugged everyone and told each other how wonderful it was to meet each other. Little had they noticed that their parents were back carrying some cold drinks.

"Made some new friends, have we?" asked their father.

"We certainly have," Ekrem and Alida replied, before pushing against the edge and gliding across the water together.

Theophilus and Kayra looked at each other and grinned.

"Ekrem's a good boy," commented Theophilus, "I think you two would get on well, Kayra."

"Alida's a lovely girl too," replied Kayra. "You'd get on well with her too."

"Looks like we're all done," concluded Theophilus. "Mission complete."

THE END

QUIZ

Can you remember which places these are?

Answer: _____

Answer: _____

Answer: _____

Answer: _____

Answer: _____

Answer: _____

Answer: _____

Answer: _____

Ekrem and Alida collected seven treasures from the
seven cities. Can you remember what they were?
Write them down below:

1.

2.

3.

4.

5.

6.

7.

Who do you think Theophilus and Kayra are?

What secrets can you remember? Which ones were most important to you?

Further reading on the seven cities mentioned in this book can be found in Revelation Chapters 2 and 3 of the Bible

Other books available by the same author:

Atalia and the Secrets at San Gimignano

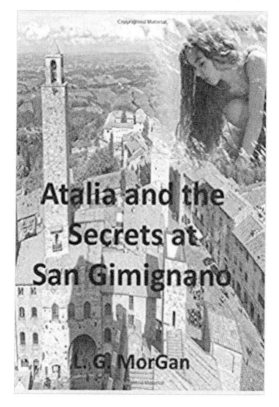

Available from Amazon

Atalia and the Secrets at San Gimignano: Amazon.co.uk:
MorGan, L G: 9781798862315: Books

Acknowledgements:

Many thanks to the incredibly photographers for providing these pictures and making them available through I-Stock and Pixabay. All pictures have been purchased and used with permission from these sites.

Thanks too to Oak Hall Expeditions who made my own experience of visiting all these sites in October 2011 possible and for all the tour guides on that trip that provided much of the information used within the book.

Printed in Great Britain
by Amazon